GEORGE WASHINGTON'S SPY

A Time Travel Adventure

ELVIRA WOODRUFF

SCHOLASTIC INC.

NEW YORK   TORONTO   LONDON   AUCKLAND
SYDNEY   MEXICO CITY   NEW DELHI   HONG KONG

This book was originally published in hardcover by Scholastic Press in 2010.

ISBN 978-0-545-10488-3

15 14 13 12   17 18 19 20/0

Printed in the U.S.A.   40
First paperback printing, May 2012

The display type was set in Caslon Antique.
The text was set in Adobe Garamond Pro.

Book design by Lillie Howard

Special thanks to Kyle F. Zelner, Associate Professor, Department of History, University of Southern Mississippi, and to Professor Robert Allison, Suffolk University, Boston, Massachusetts, for their valuable historic consultation and fact-checking of the manuscript. And to James Cross Giblin for casting an eye on the final story.

Map of Boston 1769 (pages vi–vii) courtesy of the New York Public Library

Acknowledgments

—◆✦◆—

The Mistress Martha Hewson in the story was named for a fine writer and good friend, Mistress Martha Hewson of Lansdale, PA.

Although the twenty-first-century Mistress Hewson does not admit to having any Loyalists in her bloodline, her family does hail from Massachusetts. And a more loyal friend you could not ask for.

My thanks go out to Mistress Hewson and to the other members of the Bucks County Writers Group, which include Mistress Pat Brisson, Mistress Deborah Heiligman, Mistress Sally Keehn, Mistress Susan Korman, Mistress Joyce McDonald, Mistress Wendy Pfeffer, Mistress Pamela Swallow, and Mistress Kay Winters. Each of these fine writers has been a gift to my work, and a blessing in my life.

Other Exciting Adventure Stories
by Elvira Woodruff

For Joe, my touchstone

— E.W.P.

A very special
thanks to Dianne Hess

New Plan of ye Great Town of BOSTON in New England

the many Additionall Buildings, & New Streets, to the Year

COMMON

FoxHill

Powder House

Watch House

School

Scale of ½ a Mile

BOSTON.NE. EXPLANATION.

Hill Wharf

Wind Mill Point

Beacon

Pleasant Street

CONTENTS

ONE

A Ben Franklin in Every Pocket

"THIS WILL BE OUR LAST MATH PROBLEM," Miss Howard told her fidgeting fifth-grade class. "Please turn to page forty-seven."

It was Friday. Everyone in Miss Howard's class was ready for the weekend. Matt Carlton looked down at his math book, but his eyes soon wandered from the page before him to the trees outside his classroom window. Meanwhile, Miss Howard's soft voice droned on and on.

"Three hundred and forty-six divided by . . ."

Matt stared up at the cloudless sky. How was he supposed to be thinking about math when, not long ago, he and his friends had started a club, the Adventure Club. Together they had gone on the most hair-raising adventure of their lives — back in time, to the American Revolution!

Matt looked around the classroom and saw the club's scout, Tony Manetti. He was sitting at his desk, blowing spit bubbles while crossing his eyes and balancing a pencil on his nose. In the seat behind Tony sat Q, the club's brains. He was reading a history book on his lap while the rest of his class struggled with Miss Howard's math problem. Back in the last row sat the club's strongman, big, softhearted Hooter. Hooter's real name was Brian Melrose. But after he hooted like a mother owl for an entire summer while caring for a baby owl with a broken wing, everyone began calling him Hooter. And the nickname stuck. Hooter was silently chewing off bits of his new pink eraser and spitting them through a straw at the back of Hannah Morgan's head.

Matt's friends Lily and Emma turned around in their seats and scowled at Hooter. They had no idea that Matt and his crew were part of a secret club that had traveled back in time. And that was just how they wanted to keep it. Secret.

Matt closed his eyes and vividly recalled how it felt to fight in the war against the British and Hessian soldiers, and how they nearly froze to death on the cold march to Trenton — when suddenly, a piece of eraser stung the back of his neck. Matt spun around to find Hooter giving him the thumbs-up sign and nodding toward the front of the classroom, where Miss Howard had written today's history lesson on the blackboard:

Life in Colonial America

1. What was it like?
2. How was it different from today?

Matt leaned forward in his seat and listened closely.

"Life was very different in colonial America," Miss Howard said. "Children didn't have the kinds of things you have today. If you lived back then, what do you think you'd miss most?"

Four hands instantly shot up in the air. Miss Howard blinked with surprise. "Well, nice to see you boys are paying attention. Tony, what do you think you'd miss most?"

"Electricity and cars," Tony said without hesitation. "Without electricity, people's houses were cold and really dark. And if you didn't have a horse, you had to walk everywhere you wanted to go."

"My computer," Q said without missing a beat. "Life without the Internet would be an unbearable hardship."

"You want to talk about hardship," Hooter

added. "Try life without cheeseburgers, guacamole, or toilet paper. That is real hardship."

The class giggled.

"I'm not kidding," Hooter insisted. "Not having toilet paper is no joke. And life without cheeseburgers is hardly worth living, unless you had some guacamole to eat, and they didn't."

The class roared with laughter.

Miss Howard raised her hand for quiet. "I must say, toilet paper, cheeseburgers, and guacamole is a strange combination to focus on, Brian. But historically you are absolutely correct. Diet and personal hygiene were not what they are today."

"I missed my phone," Matt said thoughtfully.

Miss Howard's eyebrows rose slowly in two perfect arches.

Matt hesitated. "I mean, I *would miss* my phone."

"Yes, they didn't have modern communication back then," Miss Howard said, smiling with approval. "Well, you boys certainly have given us a lot to think about. Now, let's go on to finish up the last of our oral reports on the Founding Fathers. Brian Melrose, will you please come up and give us your report?"

Hooter opened his notebook and began furiously paging through it. "I know I have it somewhere," he muttered. He unzipped his backpack and dug through the tightly-packed contents: books, loose papers, a half-eaten apple from lunch, a dirty pair of gym socks, a book on raising snakes for pets, and an assortment of old candy wrappers. He thought about taking a bite of the apple, but Miss Howard had begun to tap her nails impatiently on her desk.

"We're waiting," she said after another full minute had passed.

"Got it!" Hooter finally cried. He pulled out a crumpled paper that was stuffed between his dirty gym socks and a moldy bologna sandwich. He hurried to the front of the room. Then he smoothed out the wrinkles in his paper as best he could against his knee and began reading aloud.

"'Ben Franklin was the greatest Founding Father. He lived over two hundred years ago. Ben Franklin wasn't boring. Once he chased a tornado on horseback, and he loved to fly kites and tell jokes. He did many things that are still useful to us today. Because of Ben Franklin we have free libraries. Ben was a great talker. He talked the French king into helping us fight the British. He was also a great inventor. He invented many things like the Franklin stove, bifocal eyeglasses, and the lightning rod. He was generous, too. Ben never got a penny for his lightning rods. He said he didn't want money for them. He just wanted to make people's lives better. I think Ben Franklin was the best Founding Father our country ever had.' "

Hooter put down his report and dug into his pocket. He had a big grin on his face.

"My grandfather gave me money for my birthday last Saturday. It was just one bill, but guess whose picture is on it?" He pulled out a folded piece of tinfoil and carefully unfolded it. "It's Ben Franklin!" Hooter beamed, holding up a one-hundred-dollar bill for everyone to see.

"Wow!" Marco Diaz breathed aloud.

"Hooter, you're so lucky!" Sara Bender said.

"Does your mother know that you've brought that much money to school?" Miss Howard interrupted.

"Yes, ma'am," Hooter replied. "She said I could bring it in for my report, as long as I promised to keep it somewhere safe. I was going to put it in my wallet, but I thought it would be safer in the tinfoil. Nobody would think anything as important as a hundred-dollar bill would be wrapped in tinfoil."

Miss Howard frowned. "That doesn't seem like the wisest choice, but go on with your report."

" 'So, as you can see,' " Hooter continued, " 'Ben Franklin was an amazing Founding Father who cared about people and making their lives better. In honor of Ben Franklin, I'd like to make your lives better, too.' "

He reached into his backpack and pulled out a roll of green bills held together with a rubber band. "I am giving each of you a Ben Franklin to put into your own pockets. I have one hundred dollars for each of you!" Hooter grinned and waved the money in the air. He proceeded to place a bill on everyone's desk.

Matt was as flabbergasted as anyone. Hooter had never mentioned this part of his report. How had he done it? Matt wondered. Had Hooter's parents won the lottery? Had someone died and left Hooter a millionaire? Whatever it was, there was now $2,500 in crisp Ben Franklin hundred-dollar bills in Miss Howard's classroom. Everyone agreed that it was the best oral report anyone had ever given.

Matt stared down at the green bill on his desk. Sure enough, Ben Franklin's picture was on it.

"Wow, I'm going to buy an iPod!" Finn Kenney shouted. "Hooter, you're the best!"

"I'm going to buy a trampoline," announced Mia Hortez.

"I'm going to buy a monkey and teach him tricks!" Jack Hutchinson cried. "Thanks, Hooter!"

But as kids began turning their bills over, they were disappointed to find that they were all blank on the back.

"Hey, they're fake!" Marcy Chin cried out.

Soon the class was in an uproar.

"Settle down, everyone," Miss Howard ordered. She picked up the bill from Matt's desk and turned it over in her hand. "Brian Melrose, where did these come from?"

Hooter smiled sheepishly. "I sort of made them," he admitted.

"You sort of *what*?" Miss Howard asked.

"I used my dad's color copier," Hooter explained. "After my grandfather gave me a hundred dollars, I thought it would be cool to give some money to everyone."

"Good grief!" Miss Howard cried. "Don't you know that copying money is against the law?"

"It's called counterfeiting," Q spoke up. "An exceedingly illegal activity." (Q loved words, and each week he had a new favorite. This week's word was *exceedingly*, and he used it whenever he could.)

Hooter swallowed hard. "I didn't know I was breaking the law."

"Q is right," Miss Howard said. "And unless you want to go to jail for counterfeiting, Brian, each of these phony bills must be collected and destroyed this very minute. Pass them forward, guys, right now."

This command was followed by a loud chorus of moans and groans, and Hooter's wild popularity suddenly plummeted. Fortunately, Miss Howard did not have her heart set on buying a monkey, or an iPod, or a trampoline. After giving Hooter another lecture on counterfeiting and making him promise never to do it again, she gave him an A for his report.

"Now for our class assignment," Miss Howard continued. "Since we've been studying the Revolutionary War, we've studied the Patriots, who were the American colonists who revolted against British Rule.

"We've also learned that the Loyalists, who were also called Tories, were the colonists who stayed loyal to King George. There were many Loyalists living in Boston in the winter of 1776.

"The British had taken over the city, and things didn't look very good for the Patriots. But George Washington came up with a plan to outfox the British. It happened on the hills outside of Boston, in a place called Dorchester Heights. I want you to learn all you can about what happened there in March of 1776 and how it affected the Loyalists who were living in Boston. Imagine, if you can, what it must have been like to be either a Patriot or a Loyalist during that time. Then choose a side and write your paper from that point of view."

"Why would anyone want to be on the other side?" Hooter asked.

"That's what I want you to find out," Miss Howard told him. "Your assignments are due on Monday."

"Monday!" the class moaned in unison. The four Adventure Club members looked at one another in dismay. There went the weekend. How would they ever finish their assignments and still have time for the campout in Tony's backyard that they had planned for that night?

"Homework," Matt muttered under his breath. "I'd rather fight the Hessians."

"Be careful what you wish for," Q warned. "The way things are going with our club, you never know what might happen."

TWO

Marshmallows, Catapults, and Redcoats

LATER THAT AFTERNOON, ALL FOUR MEMBERS of the Adventure Club were huddled for a private meeting in a tent in Tony's backyard. Matt was so happy, he could hardly sit still. His parents were going away that weekend to attend a wedding. His pesky little sister, Katie, would be staying overnight with their friends, the Capells, who lived next door to Tony. And Matt would be spending Friday night at Tony's house with Hooter and Q.

"You really had everybody fooled with that fake money, Hoot," Matt said.

"Good thing Officer Yee wasn't in school talking about safety today, or he probably would have arrested you," Tony added.

"How was I supposed to know it was against the law?" Hooter mumbled through a mouthful of marshmallows. He licked his fingers and closed the bag.

"New sneakers again, Hoot?" Tony asked, eyeing Hooter's puffy purple sneakers.

Hooter nodded. "My mom says that this is the last pair she'll ever buy me. She said if I lose one more pair of sneakers, I'll have to pay for them myself out of my allowance or go barefoot."

"You're the only person I know who loses their shoes," Matt said.

"Why'd you take them off in the first place?" asked Q.

"I can't watch a movie with my shoes on," Hooter explained. "Besides, how was I supposed to know someone would reach under my seat and steal them?"

"Well, you don't have to worry about anyone stealing those sneakers," Matt said. "They're about two sizes too big for any of us. And they're purple!"

"I'm going to sleep with them on tonight, just in case," Hooter decided.

The others laughed, and Tony gave Hooter a friendly shove.

"It's great that we get to camp out together," Matt said. "I just wish we didn't have so much homework to do."

"It will be simple," said Q. "All we have to do is some reading and find out what happened at Dorchester and what it was like to be a Loyalist."

"Why would anyone want to be a Loyalist and not be allowed to choose their own laws?" Hooter asked.

"I don't know," Tony said. "The Loyalists must have been really stupid."

"All five hundred thousand of them?" Q asked.

"Five hundred thousand!" Matt repeated. "Are you sure there were so many?"

"Yes. And that was about twenty percent of America's population in 1776," answered Q. He dug into his backpack and pulled out the leather-bound history book his uncle had given him. "I read that in here."

"So what happened in Dorchester?" Matt asked.

"Let's look it up and read about it," said Q as he flipped through the pages.

But before he could find Dorchester, Tony pulled from his pocket the antique brass spyglass that he had bought at a garage sale for fifty cents. He opened the tent flap and pointed the glass at the big oak tree in his yard.

"Does that thing really work?" Hooter asked.

"It's got a big crack in the glass," Tony said, handing Hooter the spyglass. "But take a look at that squirrel in the tree."

"Cool!" Hooter exclaimed, looking through it. "I can see his whiskers twitching."

Everyone jumped up to take a turn looking.

"Hey, you guys," Q interrupted. "We still need to be thinking about our homework assignment."

"First we have to discuss club business," Matt said.

"How about candy? That's club business, isn't it?" Hooter asked. "We've got one bag of marshmallows, but has anyone got any *good* candy?"

Matt and Tony shook their heads no.

Q shrugged. "I'm not allowed to eat candy. My dad is a dentist, remember? Besides, the tooth is the only part of the human body that can't repair itself. That, and people's out-of-control candy consumption will pay for my college education."

"So that's a no?" Hooter sighed, his shoulders slumping.

"We've got more important club business than that," Matt told them.

"What about our homework assignment?" Q tried once again. He held up his history book. "We could read up on Dorchester in here."

"Q, the campout just started, and already you want to do homework?" Tony said, shaking his head in disgust.

"But this homework could be fun," Q said.

"About as much fun as getting a wart removed," Hooter groaned.

"Hoot's right. Tonight is for fun," Matt declared. "And I checked the weather online. It's going to get colder, so it's good we've got warm sleeping bags." Then he hesitated. "And there is going to be a three-quarter moon. . . ."

His voice trailed off and everyone grew quiet. They were all thinking of the last time they'd gone camping under a three-quarter moon. They weren't supposed to go near the lake at night. But it was on their last campout that they'd found the old boat that sent them back in time, on the most harrowing experience of their lives.

"That's not even something to joke about," Q said. "If there is a three-quarter moon, I'm staying far away from that old rowboat. I've had enough of Hessian soldiers, and redcoats, and musket balls, and—"

"And people dying," Matt said softly.

"It could have been us," Hooter added.

"And don't forget that legend my grandfather told me about," Tony said. "All those people who went out on the lake and never came back."

"Most likely they got into that old boat like we did, not knowing it was a time-travel vehicle," said Q.

"Except they never made it home," Tony whispered with a shiver. "Imagine being stuck back in time for your whole life and never seeing your family again."

"Like poor Adam Hibbs," Tony said. "He never got to come back."

"Then we all agree," Matt said. "Nobody is ever going near that boat again. We might have been killed in the Revolutionary War — or died of the pox. We can have plenty of fun right here in Tony's yard. And this time it will be a Katie-free zone."

On their last trip, Matt's little sister, Katie, had ended up going back in time with them and causing all kinds of trouble.

"Let's all have a marshmallow to celebrate." Matt grinned, snatching the bag from Hooter, and everyone grabbed one.

"Here's to staying far away from that old rowboat," Tony said.

They all tapped their marshmallows together and said, "Clink!" Then they fell over one another laughing.

Q dug through his backpack and pulled out a small book about the life cycle of the cockroach. "Did you know that a cockroach can live up to nine days without its head? The only reason they die is starvation."

"I wonder what kind of bugs they had back in colonial times," Matt said.

"It doesn't talk much about bugs in here," Q said, putting down the cockroach book and picking up his history book again. "But there are lots of things about the American Revolution in this one." He began flipping through the pages. "Plus there's some cool stuff here that isn't in our social studies book." He turned a page and held it up for the others to see. "Like spies. Did you know that George Washington had spy rings working for him?"

"Like secret agents?" Tony asked.

"Exactly," Q told him. "And without those spies, we might have lost the war."

"That's pretty cool," Matt said.

"Oh, and here is Dorchester!" Q said. "Should I read it out loud?"

"Just tell us what happened so we can get back to having fun," Hooter said.

Q scanned the page while Tony told a cockroach joke and Hooter did his impression of a skunk.

"Okay, you guys," Q called, looking up from his book. "Listen to this. General Howe was the British commander who had captured Boston. Everyone was afraid of him and his army of redcoats. They had blocked the harbor and had tons of cannons. General Washington was in Cambridge with his troops, but they were outnumbered."

"So what did they do?" asked Matt.

Q shrugged. "I haven't gotten that far. But I could read it out loud and we could find out."

"I've got a better idea," Tony said. "Why don't we put the book away and have a battle of our own?"

"Yeah, cool!" said Matt. "We can set up some of my old army men and pretend they're redcoats. We can use your catapult from the castle set you got for your birthday, Tony."

"We could bomb them with marshmallows, if Hooter stops eating them all," Tony suggested, grabbing the bag away from him.

A few minutes later, the young time travelers were laughing and joking as they loaded the catapult and took careful aim. For now, they were glad to be in their own time, dive-bombing toy soldiers and decimating armies with marshmallows, in the safety of Tony's backyard.

Meanwhile, in the house next door, a very different conversation about time travel was taking place.

THREE

Show Us the Boat

"I *DID SO* SEE GEORGE WASHINGTON!" MATT'S little sister, Katie, insisted. Katie was only seven, but she always knew how to stir up trouble. She stamped her foot, and her springy red curls bobbed up and down.

"You mean you saw him in a book," ten-year-old Emma Capell corrected her.

"Or maybe you saw him on a dollar bill," Emma's sister, Lily, added.

"No!" Katie persisted. "I saw the real George Washington."

Lily and Emma scowled. The two sisters were twins, but not identical. Although they both had long chestnut brown hair, Lily's eyes were deep brown, while Emma's were crystal blue. And their personalities were as different as the color of their eyes.

Lily was a good student and a take-charge kind of girl. She loved to run fast, ride horses, and boss everyone around. Emma, on the other hand, was an artist and a dreamer. She loved fashion, flowers, and make-believe.

On this afternoon, the girls were eating Mrs. Capell's fresh, hot, homemade chocolate-chip cookies at the counter in the twins' kitchen. Lily and Emma knew they had homework to do, too, but like the boys, they decided to put it off until later. Emma had talked the other girls into playing *Model Makeover*, her favorite TV reality show. The three wore old bridesmaids' gowns that the twins' mother had altered for them, along with her old fake fur coats. The striped tights on their legs and the scuffed sneakers on their feet made for an unusual contrast with the formal dresses. But the girls didn't mind.

"I love my dress," Katie declared. "It must have about five hundred bows on it." She happily fingered the little yellow ribbons that were sewn around the hem.

"I hate bows. I hate dresses, and I hate pink," Lily grumbled. "And this dress is the same gross pink color as cough medicine."

"You look beautiful, Lily," her mother said, coming back into the room.

"What about me?" Emma asked, stroking her flouncy lavender gown. "Don't I look beautiful, too?" She left her chair and twirled around on the floor.

"Like a princess," her mother said, smiling. "But it looks like your hem is coming undone. Let me go get my sewing box and fix it before you trip and hurt yourself. It only needs a few stitches."

"Who wants to be a princess, anyway?" Lily griped, once her mother was out of the room.

Katie took out her little pink flashlight and shone it in Lily's face. "You don't look so good," she said. "I've got some candy pills in my doctor's bag that could help."

Lily scowled as Katie dug into her pocketbook and held up a little bottle of blue candy pills.

"No, thanks," Lily said. "Those things taste like plastic."

"But they will make you all better," Katie insisted.

"No, they won't," Emma told her. "They're fake, just like your George Washington story."

"But I really did see George Washington in a boat," insisted Katie. "He gave me his socks. Matt and his friends were there with me. They're having their meeting in Tony's backyard right now. You can ask them."

The twins turned in unison to look out the kitchen window. "I don't see anybody over there," Lily said.

"That's because they're probably in Tony's tent," Katie told her.

"Why would George Washington give you his socks, anyway?" asked Emma.

"Because my feet were cold," Katie explained.

The twins' mother returned to the room with a white wicker sewing box. She threaded a needle and picked up the hem of Emma's dress. She sewed a few stitches, made a knot, and snipped it with her scissors. Just then a phone rang in the hall, and she left the room to answer it.

"I like your earrings. Are they new?" Katie asked Emma.

"Yes, Lily and I both got a pair. Don't they look like real diamonds?" She pushed back her hair to reveal the large, glittering, diamondlike studs in her ears. Lily did the same.

"Oh, my goodness!" Katie said, perking up. "Did they cost a hundred dollars?"

"No," Lily explained. "They were only six dollars, because they aren't real diamonds. They're pretend, just like your George Washington story."

"But I'm *not* pretending," Katie insisted.

"So George Washington, the first president of the United States, gave you his socks?" Lily asked.

"Even though he's been dead more than two hundred years?" added Emma. The two girls broke into peals of laughter.

Katie chewed thoughtfully on the end of her stethoscope. "He didn't look dead to me. But he did have long white hair, and he wore funny-looking clothes."

"So what did you do? Travel back in time?" Emma asked as she opened a bottle of red nail polish and began to paint her fingernails.

Katie shrugged. "I don't know. I guess so."

"How?" asked Emma. "How did you travel back to George Washington's time?"

"A boat took us there," Katie told her.

"Oh, right, a time-travel boat." Emma shook her head and smoothed down the satiny skirts that fell over her orange-and-green-striped stockings.

"They say George Washington never told a lie. And you shouldn't lie, either, Katie Carlton," Lily scolded.

"But it's not a lie!" cried Katie. "You can ask Matt."

"If it's not a lie, then where are the socks?" Emma demanded.

Katie's lower lip trembled. "I traded them with Q for some marshmallows," she said in a little voice.

"Sure you did." Emma sighed, waving her wet fingernails in the air. "Come on, Lily, let's go outside and pretend the dock is a runway."

The two sisters sprinted out the door.

"I know you don't believe me," Katie called after them. "I can't show you the socks, but I know where the boat is. It's in a secret place that only the boys and I know about."

The twins stopped and turned back around. "All right, then. Prove it," they said at the same time. "Show us the boat."

"Okay," Katie said. "I will. But first, can I have another cookie?"

FOUR

Somewhere Over the Rainbow

THE BOYS HAD JUST TORPEDOED THE LAST OF the redcoats when Tony looked back through his spyglass and saw his mother out front, walking up the driveway. Their neighbor, Mrs. Capell, was with her.

"Red alert! Red alert! Nonmembers approaching clubhouse," he whispered as the two women headed for the backyard.

"Have you fellows seen Katie and the twins?" Mrs. Capell asked.

"Nope," Matt said with a satisfied smile. "There are no girls here."

Mrs. Capell's usually sunny face suddenly darkened with worry. "I tried calling Emma on her cell phone, but she's not picking up. I wonder where they went. They should have been home by now."

Leave it to Katie to have gotten into trouble already, Matt thought.

Mrs. Capell looked down at her watch. "They were playing dress up and having a snack. Katie was talking some nonsense about a hidden boat and George Washington or something. Then they went back outside to play. But that was over an hour ago."

Matt's mouth went dry.

"Don't worry, Sara," Tony's mom tried to reassure her. "The girls know they're not allowed to go beyond the cove. I'm sure they'll be back soon."

Mrs. Capell nodded. "You're probably right." She turned back to the boys. "If you see them, please tell them to come home right away. I've got their supper waiting."

"W-w-we will," Matt managed to stutter.

"Did you hear that?" Hooter gasped when the two women were out of sight.

"Katie must have told them about the boat!" Tony exclaimed.

"We've got to find them right away!" said Matt. "And when I find Katie, she's going to be sorry."

"You mean, *if* you find her," Q interrupted. "If she and the twins found the boat, they could be anywhere in time or space."

"What if they land in the middle of a real battle?" Hooter whispered.

"We were lucky to make it back alive," Tony said. "But Katie and the girls could end up like those people my grandfather told me about, the ones who went out on the lake and disappeared forever."

Before anyone could say another word, Matt took off, and the others followed. "Katie!" he shouted. "Katie, where are you?"

But there was no reply. Matt's heart pounded as he picked up speed. The more he thought about his little sister getting into the old rowboat, the more frantic he became.

"Katie! Katie! Where are you?" Hooter echoed.

"Lily! Emma!" Q and Tony shouted.

They followed the narrow path that curved around the lake. It led them deeper and deeper into the woods. The leaf cover overhead grew so thick, it blocked out the sun. They made their way through a tangle of twisted vines and gnarly-looking trees. Even the air smelled different in here. It had a musty, wild scent. The shrill cackle of a crow, echoing through the woods, made everyone jump.

"Ow!" Hooter cried, tripping over a log and falling to his knees.

Q held his breath as he brushed a spider's lacy web from his cheek.

Matt's own face stung as branches whipped across it while he ran. But he had to keep going. He had to find Katie. His heart pounding, he raced on. Soon he heard Tony yell, "Stop!"

"What is it?" Matt shouted. "Do you see them?"

Tony shook his head. "This is crazy. They could be anywhere."

"What are we going to do?" asked Hooter.

"Why don't you try to call them," Q suggested.

Matt took out his cell phone and snapped it open. He selected Emma's number and pressed SEND. "It's ringing!" he whispered.

Beyond the bushes, somewhere in the distance, the faint tune of "Somewhere Over the Rainbow" could be heard.

"That's Emma's phone!" Matt said.

The boys ran toward the song and out to a clearing above a small cove. But as Matt looked down onto Levy Lake, he saw a sight that chilled his blood. For there in the tall weeds and shallow water were Katie, Lily, and Emma. They sat, trancelike, still as stones, in the familiar old blue rowboat!

"Katie!" Matt cried. "Katie, Emma, Lily! Get out of there! Get out now!" But the girls just stared straight ahead, their faces dazed and blank. The only sound to be heard was the plinking melody of "Somewhere Over the Rainbow" coming from the phone clutched in Emma's frozen hand.

Matt started down the hillside. "Katie! Katie!" he screamed as he ran toward the boat.

"Matt, no!" Tony cried, reaching for his arm.

"You can't go down there!" Hooter shouted, grabbing his other arm.

Matt ignored their pleas and continued pressing on toward the boat. The boys, pulled along by Matt, shouted for him to stop. But once they reached the pebbled beach, the boat silently glided beside them, beckoning them to come in. The group fell suddenly quiet under its spell.

Glassy-eyed, the four boys climbed aboard the small craft. They sat down next to the girls on the weathered old wooden seats. A blue mist rose up around them. As the craft began to quiver, a gust of wind whipped the baseball cap off Tony's head. Seconds later there were neither boys, nor girls, nor a boat to be seen.

An eerie silence followed, broken only by the sound of a wave gently lapping around the small blue baseball cap left floating on the water.

FIVE

Stuck!

THE BOAT SPUN AND SPUN AS IT WAS THRUST into darkness and space. It kept on spinning until it landed with a thud and a splash. When the darkness lifted, all seven children were bruised and lying in a tangle of arms and legs at the bottom of the old rowboat. The boat rocked back and forth as gentle waves rippled against its sides.

"What happened?" Lily asked, dazed and queasy, her eyes trying to focus. She struggled to reach out to Emma but found her friend Matt beside her instead! Hooter, Tony, and Q were under them. Emma and Katie moaned from the bow.

"Matt, what are you doing here?" Lily said faintly.

"I feel so dizzy," Emma croaked.

"My leg hurts," Katie whimpered.

"I'm freezing," Tony complained.

"Where are we? And when did you guys get into this boat?" Lily wanted to know.

"It's a long story," Matt tried to explain. "It was supposed to be our club's secret."

But Lily had stopped listening. She was too distracted by what she saw. For Levy Lake, the lake she last remembered looking at, the lake she had known all her life, was gone! In its place was a wide, icy river surrounded by fields and trees. And they were drifting along in the old rowboat between large chunks of ice.

"Where are we?" Lily asked again.

"Good question," Q said. "Though I can't guarantee that we're even in the twenty-first century." He nodded toward a building he could see in the distance. It was made of stone and had a big wooden waterwheel that splashed water against its side.

"I believe that's called a gristmill," said Q, with the authority of someone who had read his entire social studies book for fun. "They were quite popular in the eighteenth century."

"What's he talking about?" Lily asked, her voice rising with panic. "What's going on?"

"Oh, no, my phone is gone!" Matt suddenly announced. "It was in my hand when we were running down to the boat. I must have dropped it."

"Well, I've still got mine, and I'm calling home," Emma said. She grabbed her phone from her bag and flipped it open. But panic set in when the words OUT OF RANGE and NO SIGNAL lit up the screen.

"I'm freezing," Katie said, her teeth chattering loudly.

"Why does it feel like winter all of a sudden?" Emma asked.

"Because it probably is winter," Matt told them. "You see, this boat is no ordinary boat." He let out a defeated sigh as the awful reality sunk in. "It's a time-travel boat."

"What?" Lily stared back in disbelief. "You're kidding, right?"

"Actually, he's totally serious," Q said.

"But we can't be sure where in time the boat has taken us," Tony added.

The twins gave each other a frantic look. "Then Katie wasn't making up that crazy story about meeting George Washington?" Lily asked.

"No," Matt said. "He even gave you his socks, didn't he, Katie?" But as Matt looked down at his little sister, he saw a large circle of blood seeping through her tights at her ankle. "Oh, no, Katie! You're bleeding!"

Katie immediately began to sob.

Q reached into his pocket for the clean cloth handkerchief that his mother always insisted he carry. Matt wiped away Katie's tears, then tied it around her ankle. "It's a pretty bad cut," he said. Then he wrapped his arms around Katie to keep her warm.

"We've all got to get out of this cold," Emma said through chattering teeth.

"She's right," Tony said. "And once it gets dark, it's going to get even colder. We'll all freeze to death out here."

"Tony, quit exaggerating," Hooter snapped. "Okay, it's cold, but nobody is going to freeze to death. Are they, Q?"

All eyes were on Q as he adjusted his glasses. "It takes three hours," he said.

"What do you mean, three hours?" Hooter asked.

"The normal internal temperature of the human body is ninety-eight point six," Q explained. "Hypothermia occurs when the body's core temperature drops to ninety-four or less, which takes approximately three hours. And it seems exceedingly possible in this situation."

A frosty gloom descended over the group.

"Let's just hurry and get to dry land," Matt ordered. He and Lily each took an oar and began to row. Minutes later, they were nearing the river's edge when a high-pitched howl ripped across the chilled water.

"What was that?" Katie cried.

"Sounded like a cat," Matt whispered.

"My cat, Muffin, never sounded like that," whispered Hooter.

"It sounded more like a wolf," Q said, nervously adjusting his glasses.

Nobody moved as the boat drifted into the dark shadows along the water's edge. A sharp breeze whistled through the towering spruce trees along the shoreline, and another piercing howl echoed from a distance.

When the boat got to shore, the boys and the twins pulled it onto solid ground.

"Tony, you're the scout," Hooter said. "Why don't you hike over to that mill and scout around to see if anyone is in there?"

"Go out there alone? With wild wolves running around? Are you crazy?" Tony balked.

"Tony's right," Matt said. "We should probably stick together."

Katie yelped in pain as she tried to stand. "I can't walk!" she cried. "My ankle hurts too much."

Lily and Emma helped her out of the boat, but

she let out an agonized cry each time she tried to put weight on her foot.

"I think she must have sprained it," Lily said, looking at Katie's swollen ankle.

"We'll have to go for help," Matt decided. "You girls stay here with her. Just huddle together to stay warm."

The girls helped Katie over to a large log, and they held her on their laps. Just as the boys turned to leave, there was a flash of light — then a loud hissing sound. Water sprayed in a wide arc. The children spun around and watched in horror as the old blue rowboat vanished into an eerie blue mist.

They hurried back to the river's edge and looked around. They all stared in stunned silence. Without the boat, there was no way home. And the boat was nowhere in sight.

SIX

What Fool Does Not Know the Year?

"WE'LL GO AND FIND SOMEONE WHO CAN HELP us right away!" Matt cried.

"But what if something happens to you?" Emma wailed.

"Whatever you do, don't you girls leave this spot until we get back," Matt told them. "Or we may never find each other again."

"Don't go! Please don't go, Mattie-o," Katie cried. That was the name she gave Matt when she was a baby and couldn't say Matthew.

"Katie, you've got to let us go," Matt said.

"Here, take this with you, then," Katie said, handing him her little pink flashlight.

Matt shoved it into his pocket. "Don't worry," he told her. "We'll be right back."

Lily grabbed hold of his arm with a look of panic. "Promise?" she said.

"We promise," Matt answered.

Matt led the way onto a path that cut through the thick brush, with the boys following close behind. The farther they went, the denser the woods became. Tree branches creaked and moaned as they bent with the wind. There was a sudden rapid beating of wings as something flew down low, just over their heads. Matt shuddered.

The path quickly split in two.

"Which way do we go?" Hooter asked.

"I don't know," Matt said. "I don't see any houses."

Tony took his spyglass from his pocket and brought it up to his eye. He pointed the glass down one path and then down the other. "It all looks the same," he sighed.

"What do you think, Q? You've got the superior brain," Hooter said.

They waited as Q adjusted his glasses, then thoughtfully studied each path. He held up his finger, as if testing the wind. Finally, he put his hand back into his pocket.

"I say we flip for it," he announced.

"Some superior brain," Hooter grumbled.

Matt led the boys on the path to the right. They walked and walked before the stone building they had seen from the distance came into view.

They followed Matt up the wooden steps to a

narrow porch. He knocked on the wide plank door. Minutes later the door opened, and an old man with a straggly gray beard stood before them. He wore a long green coat and brown trousers that were gathered with raggedy black ribbons at his knees. His clothes stank of sweat, and rum, and something gone sour.

"The miller will do no more business this day," the old man said gruffly. "The redcoats have locked him up for taxes owed." And before Matt could stop him, he slammed the door shut!

"Did you hear the way he talked?" Matt asked, his face turning pale.

"And did you see his old-fashioned clothes?" Tony added.

Matt knocked on the door once more. "Excuse me, sir," he said when the old man reappeared. "My little sister is hurt and we need help."

The old man's eyes narrowed at the sight of the boys' colorful down vests and sneakers. "Where have you lads come from? Why are you dressed so strangely?"

Hooter was about to answer when Matt spoke up. "We're not from here. We're lost. If you could just tell us where we are . . ."

"Why, you're at Sutton's Mill a ways outside of Boston town," the old man said suspiciously.

The boys glanced at one another and cringed.

"And the date?" Matt asked. "We kind of lost track of time."

The old man glowered at him. "'Tis the end of February."

"And the year?" Matt asked slowly.

"What fool does not know the year? Why, 'tis 1776!" the old man snapped.

Matt shut his eyes tight. It couldn't be true.

"I've no time to waste on such nonsense," the old man muttered, and started to close the door.

"Wait!" Matt cried. "I need to get my sister to a doctor. Do you think you could help us?"

But the old man shook his head no. "The nearest physician was hung as a rebel spy last month." Then he looked sharply at the boys. "So tell me, are your families warm to the colonies' cause, or are they tender of the English?" His piercing green eyes seemed to look right through them.

"Our families are Americans," Matt assured him. "Americans, through and through."

"My uncle is in the army," Tony piped up. "He is the most patriotic person I know."

"Ah, Patriots." The old man's voice softened. "And what colony do you Patriots call home?"

"Nebraska," Hooter blurted out, before the others could stop him.

The old man cocked his head and ran his fingers thoughtfully through his beard. "What is this place, Nebraska?" he asked. "I know of no such colony."

"Nebraska wasn't admitted to the Union until 1867," Q whispered under his breath, stepping hard on Hooter's foot.

"We're from the west. We're not a colony yet," Q hurried to explain.

"It's getting darker and colder. And we have nowhere to stay," Tony blurted out.

"And my sister is hurt," added Matt.

"Is the girl in grave danger?" the old man asked.

"I don't know," Matt said. "She's cut her foot pretty bad."

"You'll have to look elsewhere," the old fellow barked. "And heed my advice, lads. If you know what's good for you, you'll stay far away from this mill." With that, he slammed the door shut once more.

There was nothing left for the boys to do but to turn around and go back down the steps.

"Well, we've done it again," Tony whispered. "We've gone back to the Revolutionary War!"

"And if this is February 1776, that means that we went back earlier in time than our last trip," Matt pointed out.

"Ten months earlier, to be exact," Q said, having done a quick calculation in his head, "which means the British are in Boston, and Washington and his men will soon be at Dorchester Heights!"

There was a sudden loud snapping of twigs behind them, but when the boys turned back to look, no one was there. It was then that Matt spotted a beam of light coming from a crack in a boarded-up window in the bottom floor of the mill.

"Maybe there's someone else down there who could help us," he whispered.

"The old guy made it pretty clear we weren't supposed to hang around," Hooter said.

"I'm just going to have a look," Matt said, going up to the building. He peered through a crack in the boarded-up window. "Oh, my gosh!" he gasped.

"What is it?" Hooter whispered.

"It looks like guns!" Matt exclaimed. "Lots and lots of guns! And cannons, too!"

"What are cannons and guns doing in a gristmill?" Q wondered aloud.

The crunch of footsteps again sounded behind them. Matt spun around just in time to see a rough-faced man grab hold of Q and bring a knife up to his neck! Seconds later, three other men stepped out of the shadows. There were muskets in their hands and tomahawks in their belts! They started for the boys.

"You were warned to stay away," one of the men growled. "You should have heeded that warning, and you might have lived."

SEVEN

We Are *So* Out of Range!

THE MINUTES DRAGGED ON AS THE GIRLS huddled together, trying to keep warm. The wind picked up, and dark clouds moved across the chalky gray sky. Emma kept her eyes on the river, praying that the boat would return, while Lily scanned the woods, keeping a sharp lookout for the boys.

Katie cried for her mother, then for Matt. Lily tried to comfort her, rubbing the little girl's reddened fingers in her own frozen hands. As Lily looked around at the strange, overgrown landscape, she wondered where they were and how far back in time they had gone. Everything was so strange and beyond belief, except for the numbing cold. That she knew to be real. Her fingers and toes were freezing, and Katie's nose was turning bright red before her eyes.

Lily thought about what Q had said, how a person could freeze to death in just three hours. She watched Emma flip open her phone for the hundredth time, hoping to have her signal return. But her sister's face crumpled once again at the sight of the words: OUT OF RANGE.

The loud screech of a raven echoed from across the dark water.

"What else do you have in your pocketbook?" Lily asked her sister.

"Why?" Emma asked.

"For survival," Lily told her.

"I've only got my phone and this," Emma said, holding up the bottle of red nail polish.

"Oh, great!" Lily groaned. "At least our nails will look good when we get eaten by wolves."

"What wolves?" Katie asked in a small voice.

"Don't mind her," Emma said. "She didn't mean it, did you, Lily?"

Lily saw the terror in Katie's face and was instantly sorry for what she'd said.

"Matt and the boys will be back any minute," she said, trying to smile at Katie and calm her down. Katie smiled back, but a sudden gust of wind whipped at their hair and set their teeth chattering harder than ever.

"Where could they be?" Emma wondered aloud.

"I don't know, but we can't wait out here much longer in this cold weather. We'll have to go look for them," said Lily, fear edging into her voice.

The twins helped Katie stand, and the three started for the path the boys had taken. It was slow going as they took turns carrying Katie over the rough ground. Moving quickly helped them to warm up. But the farther into the woods they went, the darker and colder it grew.

"Matt, where are you?" Lily shouted into the shadows.

"Hooter! Tony! Q!" Emma called.

The only reply was the sound of a squirrel racing over the branches of a pine tree. Something stirred in a tangle of brown vines overhead. Lily bit down on her lip and continued on until they came to the sudden split in the path.

"Please let this be the way they went," she prayed aloud, steering them to the left. They slowly made their way along the rock-strewn frozen ground. Lily was desperate to find Matt and the boys, but they were nowhere in sight. Katie groaned with each step they took. Finally, just when they thought she could go no farther, they spotted smoke in the distance! A wave of relief washed over them at the sight of the stone houses and clapboard shops that flanked a street.

But the girls soon discovered that the street was not like any they'd ever been on back home. It was not made of asphalt, but of cobblestones that were hard to walk on, and they had to navigate their way around piles of steaming horse manure.

They passed ropes and rigging that were strung before a sail shop and a bloody pig's head that hung from a butcher's iron hook outside his window. A gaggle of geese pecked at the ground, while a small boy in a blue wool coat and red cap pulled a cow by a rope. Thick smoke poured out of the stout chimneys, and the stench of ripe manure mingled with the smell of wood smoke in the frigid air.

"It looks like Star Village, that reenactment place we went to last summer with Mom and Dad," Emma said.

"Only that place had a parking lot full of cars," Lily said, nodding toward a horse and wagon tied to a hitching post.

As they neared the boy with the cow, Emma slipped her phone into her purse and called to him. "Have you seen four boys?"

The boy shook his head no and kept on walking.

Next, Lily tried knocking on the door of a house. A haggard young woman in a long dress and apron appeared at the door with a baby in her arms. Lily was instantly taken aback by the bad smells that wafted outside. "Excuse me," she said. "We were wondering if you could help us."

The woman's thick dark eyebrows arched as she looked the girls over. "I have hardly enough to feed my own children without giving away what little I have to gypsies like you. Why don't you sell the gems you're wearing in your ears if you want to eat?" And without another word, she slammed the door shut.

Lily and the girls moved on down the street, confused by the woman's rudeness.

"Push off!" they heard a man holler at some noisy geese. A squealing piglet trotted past. The man was standing with his head and hands locked in a wooden frame, his teeth chattering in the cold.

"Why is that man standing there like that?" Katie asked.

"He's in stocks," Lily told her. "We read about them in class. They used to lock people up in stocks when they did bad things and broke the law."

"What mischief are you three up to?" the man barked.

Lily took a tentative step forward. "We're looking for four boys. Have you seen them?"

"Maybe," the man replied with a cruel smile. "Maybe I saw them hop a wagon and head down this very street. Then again, maybe I didn't." As he laughed hoarsely, a stream of spittle hung from his lower lip.

Lily almost fell over backward trying to get away from him.

"Can you tell us where we are?" Emma asked.

"You're in Boston town, lass, home of the unforgiving," the man replied with a sarcastic sneer.

"And the year?" Emma pressed. "Can you tell us what year it is?"

"I may have emptied my neighbor's jug of ale, but I can still remember the yar," said the man, slurring his words. "'Tis 1776. And those cursed lobsterbacks are sleeping in our beds, stealing our food, and using our tombstones for target practice," he added with a scowl.

"Lobsterbacks?" Emma repeated.

"Redcoats!" The man spit on the ground. "The British dogs who have imprisoned us in our own city."

Lily and Emma grabbed hold of Katie and took off down the frozen footpath.

"Oh, my gosh!" Emma said, staring at the brick houses and shops around her. "Did you hear what year he said it was?"

But her words were drowned out by the sudden loud beat of a drum and the echo of boots stamping on the hard cobblestones. A brigade of soldiers in bright red uniforms came marching up the road toward them!

The girls instinctively drew back as the lines of redcoats filled the street.

"Halt!" an officer shouted.

The soldiers froze in place.

"At ease!" he said.

The men lowered their heavy muskets, and with heads tilting and shoulders sagging, they broke formation. They stood talking in small groups, when one of the men fitted his musket with a bayonet and drove it into the head of the pig that hung before the butcher's shop. He lifted the horrible-looking thing into the air and swung it around. The animal's dulled, glassy eyes stared straight ahead, and its mouth hung dumbly open.

"See here, lads," he shouted. "It's George Washington's head I've got!" His comrades roared with laughter.

"And right where it belongs, too, on the end of an English blade!" another shouted.

"Huzzah! Huzzah!" the men cheered.

The girls backed away in horror, the harsh cry of the soldiers' voices ringing in their ears. They turned down one winding street and then another, feeling as if they had been swallowed up in a labyrinth of cobblestones. A sharp wind blew back the fake fur on their coats and chilled them to the bone.

"I don't want to keep going," Katie cried, suddenly sinking down to the ground and refusing to move.

"Katie, you've got to try," Lily urged her.

But Emma sank down as well. "We don't even know where we're going."

Lily looked up at the sky. It was as bleak as their spirits, the sun rapidly sinking behind the slate-covered rooftops. It would soon be dark and would become even colder! She searched the street in a panic.

Where were Matt and the boys? What if the girls never found them? How would they survive on their own here in Boston, more than two hundred years in the past?

"Try calling home again," pleaded Lily.

"We can't," Emma sobbed, opening her phone once again. "There's no signal! We are out of range! Oh, Lily, we are *so* out of range!"

EIGHT

Moses

"PLEASE," BEGGED MATT. "PLEASE DON'T hurt us!"

But the big-muscled man coming toward him made no reply. He grabbed hold of Matt by his collar and roughly lifted him off the ground. In the sliver of moonlight that crossed his assailant's face, Matt saw that the man's eyes were hard and steely. His sallow cheeks were pitted with scars.

The man slammed Matt up against the building. Matt gasped at the pain that shot through him. Two other men shoved Hooter and Q up beside him.

"Please," Matt tried again. "Please —"

"No good begging now," the scar-faced man barked. "You've seen too much."

"We d-d-didn't see a-a-anything," Hooter stammered.

"If these spies get word back to the redcoats, they're sure to send a patrol of dragoons," one of the other men said. He fingered the hatchet that hung from his belt.

"And if we're found out, we'll all swing on the Common tomorrow at sunup," another added, pointing his gun at Q's head.

"No! No!" Matt cried. "You're wrong. We aren't spies. We're just regular kids."

"We won't tell anyone what we saw, if you'll just let us go," Q pleaded.

"We've got money," Tony blurted out. "If we give it to you, will you let us go?"

"What money?" Matt whispered.

"Hooter's birthday money," Tony said nervously, eyeing the scar-faced man.

Hooter nodded. "I was saving for an aquarium, but you can have it instead. It's a hundred dollars, and it's right here in my pocket. It's not a copy. It's the real thing. It's right there, wrapped in tinfoil, and you can —"

"Stop your jabbering," the scar-faced man barked. He reached into Hooter's pocket and pulled out the piece of tinfoil. He slowly unfolded it and held it up to show the other men. Much to the boys' surprise, their captors seemed to be more interested in the tinfoil than the money!

"I have never seen tin hammered so thin," one of the men exclaimed.

"'Tis a miracle! Why, 'tis thin as paper," another man said, rubbing his fingers over the foil.

"And look at the money," Hooter urged. "It's a hundred dollars."

"What paper currency is this?" the scar-faced man demanded on inspecting the bill.

"It's legal," Hooter hurried to explain. "See the picture on it? It's Benjamin Franklin. He's a Founding Father. I know because I did a report on him and I got an A, but I kind of got in trouble because —"

"Shut your gob," the scar-faced man shouted.

The men looked more confused than ever. "Whose father did he say he was?" one of them asked.

The scar-faced man studied the bill. He looked back at Hooter. "What trickery is this?"

"It's no trick," Hooter insisted. "That's a real one, not like the other ones I made. My teacher took all of those and —"

"Silence!" the scar-faced man bellowed. "This paper of yours is nothing but shin plaster."

"Shin plaster?" repeated Matt.

"Only good to bandage a bloody leg," the man growled. He pocketed the tinfoil but threw the bill back at Hooter. "Your worthless paper will curry no favor with us." He butted the barrel of his musket up against Hooter's chest. Then he turned to his comrades. "I say we make quick work of silencing them now, while we still have the cover of night." His fingers tightened around the gun's trigger.

"Hold your fire, man," a voice suddenly commanded.

The old man from the mill stepped out of the shadows. "You have mistaken these lads. Their kin have shed blood for our cause. And we need them alive, for they will be useful to us."

Matt's eyes met the old man's. A flicker of hope rose up inside of him. Maybe they would be saved after all. But what did he mean by "useful" to them?

The scar-faced man scowled and spit on the ground. "You'd better be right, for they waste no time on trials for the likes of us. We'll all swing if we're found out."

"No one is going to hang," the old man said firmly. "And since I am in charge, you will do as I say." He nodded to the boys. "Get them up to the mill now, and be quick about it."

The boys stumbled back up the wooden steps with muskets pointed at their backs. Once inside the mill, they huddled on the bench, while the old man ordered the other men to keep a lookout at the door.

Then he sat down on the stool and glowered at Matt. "I told you to stay away from this mill."

"I'm sorry," Matt said, squirming under the fierceness of his gaze.

"Sorry?" the old man shouted. He pounded his fist on the table. "Sorry will get you a hatchet through the heart. Sorry will get you hanged. These are dangerous times, lad, and if you hope to live through them, you must do as I say. One misstep could cost you everything. Do you take my meaning?"

"Yes, sir," Matt nodded.

The old man let out a tired sigh. "What is your name, boy?"

"Matthew Carlton," Matt replied.

The old man's eyes narrowed. "And you say you are a Patriot, Matthew Carlton? I have no proof of this, but if there's one thing I have learned in my business, it's to read the stamp of a man on his face."

"Your business being the rebel business?" Matt asked.

The old man picked up an iron rod and poked the fire. "Have you no relatives in the city?"

"No, it's like I told you. We're not from here. We're sort of . . . traveling," Matt said. "My sister came with us. She and two other girls are waiting for us back at the river."

"Well, you've chosen a most dangerous time to visit," the old man said.

"Tell me about it," Tony muttered.

"Stand up, lad," the old man said, suddenly looming over Tony.

Tony jumped to his feet.

"You'll go with two of my men down to the river and fetch the girls. If you dare to run, my men will have orders to shoot. Mind you, should they miss and you don't return, your three friends here will pay the price. Do you understand?"

Tony was so nervous he nodded like a bobble head and was quickly hustled out the door.

When the old man returned to the fire, he sank down on his stool and looked at the boys. "Perhaps we can be of use to one another," he said. "We can aid you in your search for these girls, so that you may all get home. In return, you will do us a favor."

"I don't think you'll be able to help us get back home," Matt said sadly.

"We came from really far away," Hooter blurted out.

"It's complicated," Q added.

The old man frowned. "Perhaps I'm not making myself clear. I am not offering you a choice here. The danger I spoke of is just on the other side of that door. The British are holding Boston captive and have closed our harbor. They are pillaging our homes and stealing our food. My comrades are as loyal to General Washington as any Patriots in the colonies. But they are jittery from lack of sleep and from living in the shadow of a hangman's noose. They are quick to strike if crossed."

The old man continued, "I can offer you safe passage out of here, but you must do as I say, or I'll throw you back to them. And they'll pounce, by God they will, like a hungry fox in a chicken coop. Ever seen a fox tear the head off a chicken?"

Matt's throat went dry. "I just want to find my sister and our friends and go home," he said in a shaky voice.

"Then heed my advice, lad, and you may just live to do that," the old man told him. "You say you are a Patriot? Well, you will soon have a chance to prove it." The old man walked to the door and turned back around before he left. "Oh, and one more thing. You can call me Moses."

NINE

Daughters of a Duke

"WE'VE GOT TO FIND SOMEONE TO HELP US," Lily said as the three girls slowly walked on the icy cobblestones. A horse-drawn carriage rolled past. They searched down alleys, behind wagons and carts, but there was still no sign of the boys anywhere.

Suddenly, the loud call of a bugle and the beat of a drum announced a flash of red rounding a bend.

"Redcoats!" Lily gasped, as visions of the horrible pig's head atop the soldier's bayonet came rushing back to her.

Without looking, the girls bounded away from the oncoming soldiers — and into the roar of pounding hooves and the violent clatter of wagon wheels.

"Help!" Katie shouted. Two horses pulling a coach were heading straight for her!

Emma and Lily, acting as one, lunged for Katie just in time to push her away from the oncoming horses. Tripping over Katie, the twins fell on top of her, twisting her already injured ankle. Katie let out an agonized scream.

"Whoa!" the coach driver shouted, pulling back on his reins. The horses whinnied and reared against the strain as the coach jerked to a stop. The coachman jumped down and helped the girls to their feet. Katie's throbbing leg began to bleed again, and she sobbed uncontrollably.

The coach door opened, and an elegant woman jumped out.

"Bless my soul and body!" she exclaimed, helping Lily up from the ground. "You children could have been killed!" She was dressed in fine satins, furs, and lace.

" 'Tis a miracle you are alive," the woman continued as she helped Emma to her feet. "But I'm afraid your dresses are quite soiled." She squinted as she examined their striped stockings and sneakers more closely. "Where on earth did you get such unusual clothing? What colony are you from?"

"It's a long story," Lily tried to explain.

"We don't really belong here," continued Emma. Seeing the woman's kind face, the words came pouring out. "I mean, we were just sitting on the dock together, talking —"

"We've traveled very far from our home," Lily said.

"Very far," Emma added.

"And where is your home?" the woman asked.

"We live over on Essex Way," Lily began.

"We came in the boat," Katie added.

"And we're totally lost," continued Emma.

"Oh, my stars, you've come all the way across the water from Essex?" The woman clicked her tongue. "Such a dangerous journey, for young girls to travel from England alone!"

"England?" Emma repeated. "Oh, no, we —"

But the woman interrupted them once more as she noticed the twins' sparkling earrings. Her eyes grew as round as saucers. "I can see by the jewels in your ears that you are not commoners," she said, lowering her voice. "Do tell, what is your family name?"

"Capell," Emma told her. "Our mother is Sara Capell, and our father is Earl."

"An earl! Oh, my stars, you are the daughters of Lord Capell, the Earl of Essex!" The woman gasped, stepping back and dipping into a deep curtsy. "And to think, I nearly ran you down with my coach!" Her round cheeks flushed, and she hurried to adjust her wig and her bonnet.

"You must forgive me for my untidy appearance — and for not introducing myself properly." She smoothed her skirts and curtsied again. "I am

Mistress Martha Hewson." But the distant boom of cannon fire suddenly rang through the air. "Miles away, miles away. Nothing to worry about," the woman said, looking flustered. "Now, where was I? Oh, yes, though we've been in the colonies for three generations now, my husband's family on his mother's side is quite highborn. Why, my children's bloodline, like your own, most certainly reaches back to the Crown."

"The Crown? I think you might have us mixed up with —" Lily began.

But Mistress Hewson saw Katie's bleeding leg, and she threw her arms around her. "What have we done? I'm so terribly sorry. You must allow me to make amends for this most unfortunate accident," she said. She turned and waved at the coach. "Mercy," she called. "You and your sisters come at once, and bring the blanket from the cab before these poor girls shiver to death."

Five round faces appeared at the cab's windows. "Do step out, girls, do step out!"

The cab door opened, and five young girls dressed in long, colorful capes and fur muffs spilled out of the coach in a flurry of giggles and whispers.

"Are they hurt, Mama?" asked the tallest girl, who held a roly-poly-faced baby wrapped in a woolen shawl. Another girl carried a fur-lined blanket over her arm.

"You must not catch a chill," Mistress Hewson declared as she helped to cover Katie with the blanket.

"Mind your manners, young ladies," she gently prodded her daughters. "And let us introduce ourselves properly." She waved a hand to the tallest girl, who looked to be a few years older than the twins.

"I am Mercy," the girl said. Her pretty oval face was a picture of primness. But when she smiled, two playful dimples appeared. She made a perfect curtsy. "And this is my baby brother, William."

"But we all call him Willie," the youngest of the little girls added.

"And sometimes Nilly Willy," another said, giggling.

Mistress Hewson shot her a disapproving look.

"And these are my sisters," Mercy continued. "Hope, Faith, Charity, and Patience. Patience, stop wiggling and stand still," she scolded.

Each girl smiled and curtsied as Mercy said their names. The baby squirmed in her arms, and Mistress Hewson took him from her. A short silence followed.

Emma nearly tripped as she held the sides of

her muddy dress and bent her knees, awkwardly trying to copy the curtsies the older girls had made. "I'm Emma," she said. "This is my sister, Lily, and our friend Katie." Katie tried to stand but cried out in pain.

"Oh, dear me!" Mistress Hewson exclaimed again. "I'm so terribly sorry. 'Tis all our fault. You must allow us to do right by you. My husband and I would be most honored to have you as our guests until the little one's ankle is healed. This war has taken a toll on our pantry, but God willing, our cook can still conjure up a decent pigeon pie. My husband is in the import business, and he owns several ships. We have a comfortable home on Milk Street, where you will be most welcome."

Lily glanced at Emma, then back to the woman. Katie couldn't walk. There were wild animals in the woods, and angry soldiers with guns on the streets, and the air was so cold, they feared they would freeze to death. There were no good choices.

"Thank you, ma'am," said Lily. "We'd be happy to be your guests

Emma nodded in agreement.

"Excellent," Mistress Hewson gushed. But her smile instantly disappeared at the sound of another round of cannon fire. The baby cried in her arms.

"Mama, they're getting closer," the two youngest Hewson girls whimpered as they clung to their mother's skirts.

"There, there," Mistress Hewson clucked. "Those cannons must be miles away. And besides, we've the General and his soldiers here in the city to protect us. There's no need to panic."

Though her voice was calm, Lily saw her forehead wrinkle with worry as she stole a glance in the direction of the cannon fire.

"We'd better hurry and get home," the driver told them. "Before —"

But Mistress Hewson held up her hand.

"Before what, Mama?" Faith asked as they headed for the coach.

"Before your father misses us too terribly," her mother replied. Everyone jumped at another boom of the cannon, and they quickly piled into the coach.

Before what? Lily wondered as the cannons roared again in the distance. What had the driver really meant to say? They'd better get home before what?

TEN

The Face on the Bill

MATT, Q, AND HOOTER WAITED ANXIOUSLY for Tony to return with the girls. But when the mill door finally opened again, it was only Tony who stepped inside.

"Where are Katie and the twins?" Matt cried.

"I don't know," Tony told him.

"What do you mean, you don't know?" Matt demanded.

Tony shook his head. "They weren't there, Matt! I swear to you. They just disappeared!"

Matt couldn't stop thinking about Katie and the girls. If only he hadn't left them alone. He listened to the deep, sad hoot of an owl from outside, mingled with the sound of mice scampering across the floor. The fire had died down to embers and ash, and the room was so cold that ice crystals were forming in a basin on the table.

Moses entered the mill, his arms full of wood. He set his bundle down beside the hearth and poked the embers with an iron. Then he carefully laid some twigs over the coals. Flames rose up. He added more wood, then took out his knife and pulled a short twig from the pile of kindling. He peeled back the bark at one end, shredding it and turning it into a brush. He opened his mouth and began to brush his teeth with it. Then the old man reached into his trunk and took out a small tin of loose powder. He rubbed some over his teeth.

He took a swig of rum from a pewter flask on the table, then rinsed out his mouth and spit on the floor. "Nothing whitens the teeth like a pinch of gunpowder," he said. "Though you'll have a fire in your belly, should you swallow any. Fancy some?" Moses held out the can to Q.

"No, thank you," Q replied. "I'm kind of" — he hesitated — "particular about my dental hygiene."

Moses wiped his mouth with the back of his hand and spit on the floor again. He unfolded a dirty cloth. "Oatcakes," he said, and passed them around.

Hooter grinned. "I love oatmeal cookies!" he said, cramming one into his mouth.

"They're still soft enough not to break your teeth, and they've only a thin layer of mold on them," Moses remarked, biting into one. "There's so little food left in the city, we're lucky to get these."

Now it was Hooter's turn to spit!

The old man passed around a jug of cider. Matt took a sip and winced. It didn't taste sweet like the cider he was used to. It was bubbly and yeasty and bitter. But he was so thirsty, he took a second drink, then a third. The boys scraped off the mold from their oatcakes. It was way past their dinnertime. And as Matt listened to his hungry belly rumble, he longed to be back in his own kitchen where the refrigerator was crammed with every kind of food you could think of. But he was not the only one thinking of food.

"I wonder if we'll ever get to eat a pizza again," Hooter whimpered.

"Or chocolate, or jelly beans," added Tony.

"Or marshmallows," Hooter sighed.

But Matt's thoughts of hunger were interrupted by a sudden panic. He pleaded again with the old man. "I have to find Katie and the girls before they freeze in that cold."

The old man's brow wrinkled. "You don't know these parts. With patrols of redcoats everywhere, you're likely to be picked up before you can blink an eye. That could be dangerous to you as well as to me and my men. You will have to stay here for now."

Matt fought to hold back his tears. If anything happened to Katie, he'd never forgive himself. If only he hadn't left her! What was he thinking? How stupid could he have been? If only he'd known then what he knew now.

"I know it's not easy," Moses said gently. "I, too, had a sister."

Matt raised his eyes.

"And I have a younger brother as well," the old man continued. "In fact, my friend Matthew, you remind me very much of him. Even as a child, Harry was always full of spit and fire." The old man's eyes brightened. "We spent our boyhood seeking adventure. I wish I had a shilling for every scrape he got into." Moses laughed. "Oh, he has spunk, all right, he does."

But their conversation was interrupted as a stocky old gentleman appeared at the door. Moses sprang from his seat to greet him.

"Pray, rest yourself, sir," Moses said, offering his guest the only stool.

The old gentleman took off his three-cornered hat, and with a wrinkled hand he shook the rain from it before gratefully taking the seat.

"Proud as I am of our Post Road, traveling it this time of year is not for the faint of heart," the old fellow said with a sigh. "I wager my driver was able to hit every mud hole, rut, and rubble in our path. And it has come to my attention that the coach is an invention sorely in need of improvement. I would make some calculations, if only I had the time."

"Did you have any trouble getting past the guards on the roads?" Moses asked.

The old man smiled playfully. "For a man of some girth, I can be surprisingly slippery. And I find if one carries enough gold pieces, one can be quite persuasive."

He peered over his round, wire-rimmed spectacles at the boys. "And who might these fine young men be? Their attire is most unusual."

"They are not from these parts but from the far west," Moses explained. "Their families have declared for the colonies. And so I've chosen this one to accompany me on my mission across Boston." He motioned to Matt. "He's clever enough, I'll warrant."

What were they talking about? Matt wondered. What mission had Moses chosen him for?

The old visitor shook his head and frowned. "You do realize that your clever friend here does not appear to be old enough to grow hair on his chin."

"The beauty of his youth is that the redcoats will never suspect one so young," Moses assured him.

Matt looked uneasily from one old man to the

next. What wouldn't the redcoats suspect him of? What were these old rebels plotting? And why had they chosen *him*?

"God grant that be so," the gentleman said. Then he stared down at Hooter's feet. His silver eyebrows arched high on his forehead. "What curious-looking boots!" he exclaimed, bending down to take a closer look. "Might I try one on?" he asked with a wink.

"I guess so," Hooter said, prying his foot out of his purple sneaker and handing it over to the old man.

"Such distinctive color! And the material is so unusual!" the old fellow exclaimed. He fingered the synthetic fabric with curiosity and even smelled it (but backed away when he smelled Hooter's feet). "A shoe molded for the left foot! Ingenious! And quite large for a young lad's shoe."

"I have really big feet," Hooter admitted. "Are you a shoemaker or something?"

"A shoemaker?" The old man's crinkly eyes brightened behind his spectacles, and he laughed a hearty laugh. " 'Tis been both a blessing and a curse, this need of mine to know a little about a lot."

"Surely, you are too modest, Dr. Franklin," Moses protested. "What with all of your many inventions and accomplishments."

"And yet not accomplished enough to cobble my own shoes," the old man quipped, looking down at his worn leather shoes.

At the mention of the old man's name, Hooter slipped the hundred-dollar bill from his pocket. He looked down at the bill and then back up at the man. He silently passed the bill over to Matt.

"No way!" Matt gasped under his breath.

Q and Tony leaned over Matt's shoulder. They, too, looked from the bill to the old man's face and back again.

"Way!" Hooter whispered. "It's definitely him! It's definitely Ben Franklin!"

ELEVEN

Twenty Lashes

HAPPY FOR A WARM PLACE TO SPEND THE
night, Katie and the twins scrambled into the coach.
But nothing could have prepared them for the long,
uncomfortable ride across town to the house on Milk
Street. They crowded onto the hard seats next to
Mistress Hewson. Her five daughters and her infant
son sat across from them. There they were tossed
and jolted on the springless seats as they bumped
along over the cobblestones. The sharp winds bit at
their faces through the open windows.

But as uncomfortable as they were, Lily and
Emma couldn't take their eyes off of the passing
landscape outside the coach window. Boston in 1776
was not like any city they had ever seen.

There were neither cars, nor traffic lights, nor
sidewalks. Instead, they passed horses and mules
pulling wooden wagons, carriages, and carts. In the
distance the soldiers' drums sounded.

"I must apologize for the condition of our coach," Mistress Hewson said. "The windows were smashed by an unruly mob outside our house a fortnight ago. We are having them replaced. Of course there is a wait, for Lucas and Paddock are the finest coach makers in Boston," she boasted. "Though I'm sure your father's coach is far finer, with velvet cushions and brocade drapes, I expect."

"Actually, we just have a normal Toyota," Emma answered, then she cringed when she realized she should not have mentioned their brand-new modern-day car.

"Yes, of course," Mistress Hewson said, trying to look as if she understood, for she did not want to appear foolish. She pulled a small wooden pick from her silk bag and used it to scratch under her heavily curled white wig. They bumped along, going up one narrow street and down another, when the driver slowed behind a man pushing a large cart.

The Hewson girls sat in polite silence until the youngest noticed Emma's hands.

"Look at her fingernails. They're all red!" she cried out.

Mistress Hewson leaned over to look, along with her other daughters. "Oh, my stars!" she exclaimed. "I've never seen anything like it! Whatever have you done to get them so red?"

"I painted them to match my toenails," Emma tried to explain.

"Your toenails! You paint your toenails, too?" Mistress Hewson cried.

"Yes, all girls and ladies paint their nails where we come from," Emma assured her.

"We are so cut off here in the colonies," Mistress Hewson complained. "It takes ages for anything new to finally reach us. I must ask my dressmaker at once if she can get me some of this new nail paint."

Lily watched out the window as a crowd milled about a raised wooden platform in an open field. The coach came to a sudden stop, and the driver jumped down.

"What is it, James?" Mistress Hewson called out the window.

"The street is closed, ma'am. The guards are not letting anyone through," the driver replied.

The color drained from Mistress Hewson's face. "I pray 'tis not another angry mob."

"They do not look angry, Mama," Mercy said, nodding to the people peacefully gathering in the field.

"May we get out and walk about, Mama?" little Patience pleaded, kicking her feet against the seat.

"Certainly not," her mother replied. "How many

times must I tell you? The streets are far too danger-ous in these times."

"But we'll have to wait in the coach for ever so long. And I'm bored," Patience whined.

"Lord knows how I thought to give you the name of Patience, when you are the most impatient child I have ever known." Her mother sighed. "We'll wait right here. For even if it is a peaceful gathering, with the pox going around the city, one can never be too careful."

"Did she say *pox*?" Emma whispered.

Mercy nodded. "Why, we hear more hammer-ing from the coffin makers than from the shipyards these days," she said.

Lily and Emma had read in school all about the smallpox epidemics of colonial America. They knew how fast the disease spread, and how it killed entire families. And they knew there was no vaccine yet in 1776 to prevent it.

"The sooner we get out of here and get home, the better," Lily whispered to Emma.

"Pray tell, good sir, what are all these people doing on the Common at this hour?" Mistress Hewson called out to an old man who was walking next to the carriage.

"They've come to watch the public floggings, madam," he told her.

The crowd's attention suddenly turned to the platform as a thick-muscled man in a leather apron climbed the steps. He set down a bucket with one hand and held a long black whip in the other. Lily squeezed her eyes shut at the loud *crack* of the man's whip as he snapped it in the air.

"Who is to be flogged?" a woman called out.

"Four thieves. Three caught stealing wood for their fires, and one for stealing a goose," the man answered.

"How many lashes?" someone shouted.

"Twenty apiece. They're getting off easy today."

"What's in the bucket?" a young boy in the crowd wanted to know.

"Saltwater to throw on the prisoners' wounds," a woman answered. "A strong medicine they're not likely to forget."

"That's the King's cure for you," a young man shouted. "First he taxes us to within inches of our lives, then he fills our city with his soldiers, closes our port, leaves us to starve and freeze, and punishes us when we try to stay warm."

"You best keep those thoughts to yourself, lad, unless you want the redcoats to add some stripes and salt to your own back," an old woman beside him shouted back.

"Are they really going to whip them just for

stealing food to eat and wood to stay warm?" Lily asked.

"I'm afraid so. They have broken the law," Mistress Hewson replied. She reached for the baby, who had begun to fuss and cry in Mercy's arms.

"Father says that if the laws are not obeyed, the city will fall into the hands of criminals, and no one shall be safe," Hope added.

The crowd suddenly parted to make way for a group of soldiers marching in step in their crisp red uniforms. As the soldiers passed, the crowd pressed forward, eager to get a better look at the prisoners, who were being pulled along by two ropes. There were three men and a young girl of twelve or thirteen.

One of the men in the crowd began to jeer. "Stole a goose for your dinner, aye, missy? Well, now you'll pay the price!"

"We haven't all day," another shouted. "Let's get on with it. Get them up to the post and give them their due."

There was a jerk on the rope, and the girl gasped as she and the other prisoners were pulled through the crowd and up to the platform. A wave of whispers followed in their wake. Emma hid her eyes, and Lily watched as the girl and the other prisoners were tied to a post.

"Won't someone do something to stop them?" Lily asked.

But Mistress Hewson hugged her baby close. "You children shouldn't have to witness such things."

"I wish Papa were here with us," Charity whimpered.

The driver returned to the window. "They've opened the street, ma'am."

"And none too soon," Mistress Hewson said, looking back at the crowd.

Lily's eyes were fixed on the platform. She watched the man in the apron raise his whip. She saw the girl's thin shoulders stiffen. The crowd swayed back with a collective gasp. Lily swallowed hard. She shut her eyes tight. The whip cracked, and a piercing scream ripped through the chilled afternoon air. The crowd went deadly silent. There was another loud *Crack* of the whip, followed by another bloodcurdling scream. Katie put her hands over her ears and began to cry.

"That's two," someone shouted. A ripple of whispering swept through the crowd.

Lily felt her stomach turn. She wanted to scream herself. She wanted to scream, "Stop! You have to stop!" Instead, she saw the man raise the whip over his head once again. The people in the crowd held their breath.

"'Twould be better for you young ladies not to look out the window," Mistress Hewson said in a trembling voice.

Lily and the girls instantly lowered their eyes to the floor. But there was no getting away from the continuous *Crack! Crack! Crack!* of the whip and the screams that followed. One was more heart wrenching than the next, until the horses began to canter and the loud clatter of wheels over cobblestones finally drowned out the horrible sounds.

Shaken into silence, Lily squeezed close to her twin on the seat. Emma's face had gone as white as Mistress Hewson's wig, and Katie was still sobbing beside her. Little Patience had begun to cry as well.

It had been such an exhausting day. Lily closed her eyes wearily, then immediately realized her mistake. Frantic, she looked back out the window. It was too late! For now they were miles from where they had started, and the three girls, distracted by all that was around them, had forgotten to watch where they were going.

Lily clutched Emma's arm and whispered in her ear, "We've lost the boys! Now we'll never remember how to find where they left us!"

TWELVE

Ben Franklin's Boots

BACK AT SUTTON'S MILL, MATT AND THE boys sat mesmerized before the famous Founding Father.

"Are you really *the* Benjamin Franklin?" asked Hooter. "The one who discovered electricity, and lightning rods, and the Franklin stove?"

The old man smiled contentedly at the recognition. "I can assure you, I am the real and ancient article, complete with bad knees and bunions." He kicked off his silver-buckled shoes with a grunt and wiggled his toes in his white stockings. "Ahhh, that's so much better," he sighed.

"Your face has become well known throughout the colonies, sir," Moses said.

Dr. Franklin nodded. "Yes, I've even had the dubious distinction of having my likeness painted on a chamber pot, can you believe it?" He chuckled merrily at his own joke. "I've thought of wearing a disguise, but if I did, it wouldn't be that of an over-weight old man, I can promise you. Nay, I'd prefer a more dashing look. Ah, the mischief I would make disguised as a young rake."

"Do not let Dr. Franklin's modesty fool you," Moses told the boys. "He makes plenty of mischief, and to the good of all the colonies."

"I know, I know," Hooter gushed. He leaned so far forward, he almost fell into Ben Franklin's lap!

Dr. Franklin raised his hand, as if to wave away any compliments. "Many have given much more than I in this struggle of ours," he insisted. "I fear the liberty we seek will cost us dearly, for the Crown is a mighty foe."

"The King has said that blows must decide. But little does he know how tight a fist we colonists can make," Moses said. "If only the blasted Tories would see reason and come over to our side. We could unite as one against the Crown's might and end this bloody fight once and for all."

Dr. Franklin's face clouded. "There's little hope for that now, I'm afraid. My own son has taken sides against me to favor the King. The divide cuts into my very heart." He looked away, and when he looked back, his voice rose with anger. "We must regain Boston from Howe, for 'twould send a message across the sea that America is no squawking, ill-mannered child to be punished and put over King George's knee."

Moses nodded in agreement. "If our General Washington is to outfox Howe, he'll need to know what the redcoats are planning."

"Ah, there's the rub," Dr. Franklin said. "How to get such information." He looked at Moses with a mysterious glint in his eye. "It takes a brave man to walk into the lion's den."

"It is good to have you back in the colonies, sir," Moses said with a smile.

Dr. Franklin shook his head. "In truth, I expected to retire to my books and my studies by now, but I find that Sam Adams and General Washington have other plans for me."

"You've had word from the General, then?" Moses asked.

"Aye, 'tis why I've come under cloak of the strictest secrecy. My butler back in Philadelphia has instructions to inform all of my callers that I've taken to my bed with a bad case of the gout." Dr. Franklin chortled. "Old age offers one so many unpleasant excuses to choose from."

"You've come with a plan?" Moses asked.

"I've come with something useful," Dr. Franklin answered as he reached into his vest pocket and took out a tiny rolled-up piece of parchment. He unrolled the paper and handed it to Matt. "Now, my boy, tell me what you see written there."

Matt looked down at the piece of paper. He turned it over, but there was nothing written on either side. "I don't see anything," he said finally, handing it back.

Then Dr. Franklin held the paper over the lamp's flame. As Matt and the others looked on, a message in brown ink slowly appeared.

Dr. Franklin's face shone with a boyish merriment. "'Tis called invisible stain! I came across it in my travels through Europe."

"Invisible ink! That's so cool!" said Matt.

"Cool?" Dr. Franklin repeated. "Nay, the paper is not cold at all. But the hour grows late, and we've urgent business to discuss." He guided Moses to a far corner of the mill.

Matt and the boys watched as the two old men put their heads together, whispering back and forth.

What were they saying? Matt wondered. What were they plotting?

Finally, the two men returned to the fire. Dr. Franklin sat on the stool. But they had hardly had time to get comfortable when a young coachman burst into the mill. His face was deeply pitted with scars. "We best make haste to get back to Philadelphia, Dr. Franklin," he said. "'Tis a long journey, and if the weather should turn against us, we'll be further delayed."

"Yes, Samuel, I'm coming." Dr. Franklin nodded. But as he slipped his foot into his shoe, he cried out in pain. "Blast these bunions! My shoes are insufferable."

Then, spotting Hooter's sneaker on the table, his bushy eyebrows arched. He picked up the sneaker and turned it over in his hand.

"Might I interest you in a trade, young man?" he asked.

"A trade?" Hooter repeated. "What kind of trade?"

"Your boots for my shoes," Dr. Franklin said. He held out one of his leather shoes to him. "The buckles alone are worth a pretty penny, crafted by a silversmith named Paul Revere. His work is well known in the colonies. You may have heard of him."

Hooter almost fell off his seat! He quickly wiggled his foot out of his other sneaker and handed it over. The famous man slipped his feet into Hooter's enormous purple sneakers, and a contented grin spread across his face. They were a perfect fit!

"Gadzooks!" Dr. Franklin cried, standing up. "I feel as if I'm walking on clouds! Why, what is this material?" he asked, touching the scratchy flaps.

"Velcro," Hooter replied, showing him how it worked.

Dr. Franklin burst into peals of laughter at the funny ripping sounds made by the Velcro. He opened and closed the flaps over and over, giggling each time it made the sound.

"If you please, sir!" Samuel exclaimed. "We mustn't tarry."

Dr. Franklin put his hand on the man's shoulder. "A word of advice, my young friend. He that can have patience can have what he will." Then he looked back down at his new sneakers, which he couldn't stop admiring. "Why, these boots are so comfortable, I'm tempted to walk back to Philadelphia in them!" The men in the room roared with laughter.

Then he tipped his hat, winked owlishly at Hooter, and happily strutted out the door in his new purple "boots."

When the door closed, Moses walked past the elated Hooter and turned to Matt. "In four days' time, you and I will be taking a trip across the city."

"Four days?" said Matt. "But we can't stay that long. We have to find my sister and our friends. We've got to find them right away. We left them out in the cold. They are waiting for us to return."

"You've got to do as you are told," the old man reminded him sternly.

Matt stiffened.

"The boys will wait here for you in the mill," Moses continued. "If all goes well, you'll be free to go on your way. Here, put this coat on. That strange clothing of yours will draw too much attention." Moses handed Matt a large woolen jacket with wooden buttons.

"It looks awfully big," Matt complained, holding up the extra-long sleeves.

"Roll up the cuffs," Moses told him.

Matt slipped the coat over his down vest and rolled up the cuffs. "Where are we going?"

"We will travel as teacher and student," Moses replied. "That is all you need to know."

"What if we make a mistake, and someone finds out we're not who we're pretending to be?" Matt worried aloud.

The old man's face darkened. His voice was low and deliberate. "There is no room for mistakes. The redcoats will hang us at sunrise if there are. We'll not even be laid in hallowed ground. They'll throw our bodies into a common grave." His fiery eyes met Matt's horrified gaze. "No mistakes, lad. There can be no mistakes."

THIRTEEN

Playing Colonial

MERRY CHATTER SPILLED OUT OF THE HEWSON sisters' bedroom in the elegant brick house on Milk Street. Everyone was excited to have exotic new "British" houseguests. Petticoats, ribbons, and lace shawls flew about as the Hewson girls dressed for dinner.

The twins and Katie shivered before a small fireplace in the next room as they washed up in a basin of cold water.

"Katie," Lily whispered. "You've got to play a game with us while we're here."

"What kind of game?" Katie whispered back. "I like games."

"We are all going to pretend that we're old-fashioned people, like the Hewsons," continued Lily. "Do you think you can act colonial?"

Katie nodded happily.

"Good," said Lily. "Because if you tell them that we're from the future, they'll think we're witches.

And you know what happened to people who were convicted of witchcraft in Salem, don't you?"

Katie's eyes grew round. "No. What happened?"

Emma gave Katie a sharp stare. "They did horrible things to them. You don't even want to know."

Katie gulped.

"So we have to try and fit in here. Okay?"

"Okay," Katie agreed.

But pretending to be from the eighteenth century was not so easy. When they walked into the Hewson girls' bedroom, Katie spotted the handle of a flowered ceramic bowl sticking out from under the bed.

"Look at that pretty bowl," Katie said, sliding it toward her. The Hewson girls watched in horror.

"Eww, it smells bad!" said Katie, making a face. "It looks like someone —"

Lily clapped her hand over Katie's mouth as Mercy quickly pushed the object farther under the bed with her foot.

"What is that bowl for, anyway?" Katie continued, bending down to take another look. Lily grabbed her arm and pulled her back.

" 'Tis a chamber pot, of course," Mercy answered, blushing.

"They use it at night as a toilet," Lily whispered in Katie's ear. "And we'll have to use it, too. Bathrooms haven't been invented yet."

"Why do you act so strangely?" Patience asked.

"You don't seem at all like the English girls we know," Faith added.

"That's because" — Lily hesitated — "because we have spent a lot of time out of England," she said truthfully.

The Hewson girls chattered on excitedly about their strange guests who didn't know what a chamber pot was.

"Mother told us to find you each a dress for supper," Faith said as she opened a tall wooden wardrobe and took out a satin dress. "I thought you would fancy this gown, for it matches your lovely blue eyes," she declared, holding it out for Emma to try on.

Emma was delighted to wear a real colonial gown. She quickly wriggled out of her mother's old bridesmaid's dress, and the twins watched as the Hewson girls stared in amazement at Emma's underwear.

"What's wrong?" Emma asked, seeing the incredulous looks on their faces.

"What is that strange linen you're wearing?" Patience spoke up.

"And who painted those little hearts all over them?" asked Charity.

"It's just normal underwear," Emma told her, covering herself up with her dress.

"Underwear?" said Faith. "What a funny word. What is it for?"

"Well, what do you wear under your clothes?" asked Emma.

"Nothing," said Hope.

"Except for our stays — and petticoats, of course," Mercy answered. She handed a stiff corset to Emma. "You can borrow these stays while you're here." She and Hope wrapped the cotton corset fitted with strips of whalebone around Emma's waist. She gave the strings a sharp tug from behind.

Emma gasped. "I can't breathe!" She held on to a nearby chair to keep from falling over. But when the girls slipped the dress over Emma's head, she couldn't help but marvel at how tiny her waist had become and how straight and erect she was suddenly standing.

"You should see the dress that Mama is wearing to the ball at Mrs. Lorring's house on Saturday," Hope bragged. "She had it made special for the occasion. The silk came on one of Papa's ships last spring."

Lily looked surprised. "Your parents are going to a ball? But there's a war on!"

Hope nodded. "Papa says the soldiers need entertaining now more than ever to keep their spirits up. They say that Mrs. Lorring has hired the best harpsichord player in the colony to play for them."

"And they will have the most lovely cakes and sweets," said Patience.

"The General and all of his officers will be there," added Faith.

"And everyone knows how much the General loves to dance," Hope said, spinning around the room.

"Do you mean General George Washington will be there?" Emma asked.

The girls looked surprised by the question but then started to giggle.

"Emma, you are so witty! I nearly mistook your joke for seriousness." Mercy laughed. "Of course we'd all love to see General Washington dancing at the ball. Dancing in leg irons, that is." The Hewson girls fell into peals of laughter at Mercy's joke, while panic began to rise in Lily and Emma.

The Hewson girls were making fun of George Washington! The Hewsons were a Loyalist family!

"You must tell us all about England," Faith insisted.

"Yes, what kinds of birds do you have there?" little Charity asked.

"Oh, who gives a fig about birds?" Hope chided. "I'd rather hear about the Earl of Essex's house. Is it very grand?"

"Oh, yes, do tell us about your house back in Essex," pleaded Patience.

"Our house?" the twins squeaked in unison.

"Oh, they have the biggest and best house in the whole neighborhood!" Katie chimed in with delight. "It's right on the lake. They have a flat-screen TV and two bathrooms. And they have Ping-Pong, and a swing in the playroom, and —"

Lily pinched Katie hard.

"Ouch!" squealed Katie.

"Pray tell us, Katie," coaxed Charity. "What is a flat-screen TV?"

"And what is a bathroom?" asked Faith.

"Oh, Katie makes up words all the time, doesn't she, Lily?" Emma giggled nervously.

"All the time," agreed Lily, rolling her eyes. "She *loves* to make things up."

As the girls' conversation dodged in and out of dangerous territory, Mistress Hewson sailed into the room with a great swoosh of her many silk skirts and a cloud of spicy scents. Her everyday wig had been replaced by another, taller model that had a mountain of white curls heavily powdered and perfumed with cinnamon and cloves.

Katie coughed.

"Well, well, just look at you!" Mrs. Hewson cried, clasping her hands. "What a difference a ball of soap, some water, and a fine frock can make. There's certainly no mistaking your pedigree now."

The twins stared hard at Mistress Hewson, now that they knew she was a Tory. They no longer felt quite as safe and protected as they had moments ago.

"Katie," Mistress Hewson cooed. "You must stay off of your bad foot for a few days. Charity and Patience, you may stay up here and keep her company. I'll have a tray of food sent up for you three."

"Oh, yes," Patience said, clapping her hands.

"Mama, Mama," Charity cried out. "Katie told us all about their house. 'Tis on a lake with a Ping-Pong TV and a flat-screen bathroom."

Lily and Emma braced themselves for the questions that were sure to follow. But luckily Mistress Hewson wasn't paying much attention to her youngest daughter.

"Yes, yes, my pet," she gently scolded. "What did I tell you about chattering on so? A fine lady knows how to keep still."

Startled, the twins looked with longing at Mistress Hewson on hearing her call her daughter "my pet." For it was the same expression their own mother so often used when speaking to them. She may have been a Tory, but she acted like any other mother.

"I've written a letter to your father in England," Mistress Hewson informed the twins. "We will anxiously await his reply."

The girls stopped cold at this news.

"Of course, in good times it would take only four months to reach us, but with the harbor as restricted as it is, well, it could take much longer," Mistress Hewson continued.

The twins exhaled. Of course, telephones and e-mail were centuries away! It could take months rather than minutes to reach someone across the ocean.

"Until then," Mistress Hewson went on, "I hope you will accept our hospitality and think of us as your family here in the colonies. 'Tis lucky you found yourselves a good Tory family to look after you."

Then, on seeing their troubled faces, Mistress Hewson added, "There, there, my dears. You needn't worry. Those ruffian rebels and their revolution will soon be put down, and order shall be restored to His Majesty's colonies. You'll see."

Lily didn't need to speak to her twin to know exactly what she was thinking.

They were staying with the Loyalists! And they had to find Matt and the boys right away! But first, they had to make it through dinner with the enemy.

FOURTEEN

Supper, Tongue, and Saved by the Pox

LILY AND EMMA SLOWLY FOLLOWED THE Hewsons down to the dining room.

"What if they ask us more questions about Essex?" Emma whispered fearfully.

"We just have to figure it out as we go along —" Lily told her. "— and hope they've never been there themselves."

"Hurry now, girls," Mistress Hewson called to them. "For I've asked our neighbor, Mistress Streep, to join us. She can't wait to meet you. She's from Essex, too!"

Lily and Emma felt the blood drain from their faces as they followed their hostess to the table. The Hewsons' house, though uncomfortably chilly, was elegantly furnished. Brightly embroidered tapestries hung on the wood-paneled walls, while crystal glasses and silver serving dishes sparkled in the candlelight. But in spite of the fine furnishings, there was a strong fishy odor that hung in the air. No one seemed fazed by the smell or the cold.

Mistress Hewson and her husband sat at opposite ends of a long mahogany table. The twins and the Hewsons' three eldest daughters were seated on one side. On the other side sat an older woman with a beaky, birdlike face and a tall white wig that swirled like a dollop of meringue atop her head. A young butler with a wig that was twice the size of his head stood at attention before the sideboard.

"It pleases me greatly to introduce you to my husband, Master Hewson, and our good neighbor, Mistress Streep," Mistress Hewson gushed. "I'm most pleased to present the daughters of the Earl of Essex, Lily and Emma Capell."

Mistress Streep eyed the twins before tipping her meringue-topped head in a greeting. Her eyes rested on the twins' glittering earrings.

Master Hewson rose from his seat and bowed politely. He was short and stocky. And like Lily and Emma's own father, he had kind eyes and a ready smile. But unlike Mr. Capell, who loved to wear his baseball cap and sweatpants, Master Hewson wore a white pigtailed wig, a blue velvet waistcoat, and matching trousers that stopped at his knees. He wore white cotton stockings and black shoes with silver buckles.

The twins sat down at the table, and everyone bowed their heads as Master Hewson said grace. When he finished his prayer, the young butler approached Lily. Seeing that his wig was on crooked, Mistress Hewson glared at him and coughed loudly until he straightened it.

"Madeira, miss?" he asked, holding a carafe of wine on a tray.

"What's that?" asked Emma.

"'Tis Portuguese wine, of course, miss," the butler replied.

"Oh, no, thank you," Emma told him. "I'm only ten. But I'll have a Coke."

Lily kicked her twin under the table, and Emma sat bolt upright.

"We'll just have water, please," Lily corrected her sister.

"Water?" repeated Mistress Hewson. "Why, 'tis such a poor, thin fluid with no substance. I've never known anyone here in the colonies to drink it at the table."

"I'm sure we never drank it in Essex, either," Mistress Streep added with a sharp look.

Lily's heart raced, realizing the mistake she had made. What else would they get wrong?

"You must excuse our meager table," Mistress Hewson apologized, seeing her young guest's uncomfortable look. "With the war on, our cook is hard pressed to find a leg of mutton or a joint of beef. I'm afraid we've only cod, grateful pudding, and tongue to offer you tonight."

Emma frowned at the sight of the meat on her plate. How could anyone eat tongue?

Lily tried a spoonful of the pudding and was glad to find that it tasted very much like the sweet, creamy corn pudding her grandmother often made.

"With the colonies in such turmoil, our dinners have suffered greatly. There are so many shortages. But I must say, your house tonight is one of the brightest lit on the street," Mistress Streep said approvingly.

"Mother saves our spermaceti now for special occasions," added Mercy.

"Spermaceti?" Emma repeated.

"Yes, 'tis the oil made from the sperm whale. Everyone knows that," said Faith.

That explained the room's fishy smell. But Mistress Streep began to stare strangely at the girls.

"Surely you must burn the spermaceti in your lamps back home in Essex?"

"Oh, yes, of course," Lily replied, her mouth full of pudding. "We burn whale oil all the time." She scratched an itch on the tip of her nose.

Mistress Streep's left eyebrow shot up, and the Hewson girls looked equally shocked by Lily's unladylike gesture.

"About your journey," Master Hewson broke in. "With the harbor so restricted, I am surprised you were able to make it to shore at all."

"Well, we sort of came in the back way," Lily replied, trying to look away from the untouched tongue on her plate.

Mistress Streep gave the twins a sideways glance. "I am sorry to say I am not acquainted with your family."

Lily lowered her eyes and nervously ate another spoonful of her pudding.

"But tell me how it is that you young ladies have come to travel so far without an escort?" asked Master Hewson.

Lily took a deep breath. "What I'm going to tell you is the truth," she began.

Master Hewson nodded. "Always a wise choice."

"The truth is, we weren't supposed to get into the boat at all," Lily admitted.

"You mean to say your parents don't know of your whereabouts?" Mistress Hewson exclaimed. "They have no idea that you are here in the colonies?"

"They don't have a clue." Lily sighed.

"I wish they were here with us right now," Emma said, her lip trembling. "They're so far away — so very far. . . ."

"Oh, my stars! You poor lambs!" Mistress Hewson ran over and hugged them both. "I can only imagine how you must miss your dear mother."

The twins burst into tears.

"Perhaps Papa could play a song to cheer our guests," Hope suggested.

"I should be happy to," her father said. He was about to reach into his waistcoat pocket for the pennywhistle he always kept there when his wife's stern look stopped him cold.

"Play music at the table?" she exclaimed. "Why, Master Hewson, whatever has come over you? I'm quite sure our guests would find such a display most impolite." She smiled nervously at the twins. "You must forgive my husband. His fondness for music can be quite unreasonable at times."

She proceeded to fill the awkward silence that followed with her own chatter about the upcoming ball and the "many fine people" who would be attending. The candles were nearly melted down to their candlesticks when Mistress Hewson excused her daughters from the table. "Go on up and entertain poor little Katie. I do hope her ankle heals quickly. And check on the baby as well," she said.

"We'll go with you," Lily and Emma offered as they scrambled to get away from Mistress Streep.

"But you've hardly touched your food," Mistress Hewson objected, guiding them back to their seats. "I'm afraid we've kept you both talking so much you haven't had time to eat. Please do stay and finish your meal."

"Yes, please, do stay," Mistress Streep replied with a sharp glint in her eye. "'Tis not often we get to dine with such esteemed company." She drew out the words "esteemed company" so long that Lily's heart skipped a beat.

As they watched the Hewson girls leave the table, the twins knew that there was only one way out of the dining room. They would have to eat the tongue!

"Your accent is most unusual," Mistress Streep remarked, staring straight at them. "I must say in all my years in England I have never heard such an accent as you girls have." Then she looked through the corner of her eye. "In these dangerous times, there are so many impostors going about looking to steal the very linen off your beds. Why, you just can't be too sure. Of course, that kind of riffraff will end up at the whipping post. They always do."

Lily almost choked on her mouthful of tongue. The fork slipped from Emma's trembling fingers, hitting her plate with a loud clatter. All eyes were on them when Mercy rushed back into the dining room.

"Oh, Mama," Mercy cried. "Do come quick! 'Tis Patience! Her face is flushed, and she's burning up with fever!"

Mistress Hewson flew from her seat and followed Mercy out of the room. Meanwhile, Mistress Streep covered her nose and mouth with her napkin. "Fever? In this house!" she exclaimed. "Good God, boy, don't just stand there!" she screamed at the butler, who had backed away from the table. "Go out and tell my driver to bring up my carriage at once."

"I beg you to remain calm, my dear Mistress Streep," Master Hewson said, getting to his feet.

"Calm? Only a fool would stay calm with pox in his house!" she shrieked, hurrying for the door.

Master Hewson looked at the twins and smiled a tight smile. "Silly woman, jumping to conclusions," he said. But Lily could see that his eyes weren't smiling. His eyes were not smiling at all.

FIFTEEN

Look Out, King George!
Here We Come!

MATT AWOKE THE NEXT MORNING TO A tickle on his cheek. He opened his eyes to find himself face-to-face with a small brown mouse! It turned and squeezed itself into a small chink in the wall.

It took Matt a moment to remember where he was. But as soon as he saw Tony, Hooter, and Q curled up beside him in the cold, dark mill, it all came flooding back to him.

Where were Katie and the twins? How was he ever going to find them? What kind of danger were they in?

These questions haunted Matt as he and the others spent the next three days under the rebels' strict and watchful guard. Although the mill was icy cold, Moses built fires when he could. But food was another matter.

The boys were hungrier than they'd ever been in their lives. Their meals consisted of moldy oatcakes and cheese for breakfast and moldy oatcakes for lunch and supper, with the occasional dried apple or onion.

Hooter took to daydreaming aloud about tacos, guacamole, and French fries, while Matt and Tony played game after game of tic-tac-toe on the dusty windows. Q made a thorough inspection of the grindstone and tried to calculate the amount of grain the miller could grind per day.

But the boys' attempts to distract themselves were tempered by an unspoken fear. At the end of each day, as the sun sunk behind the trees and the mill grew darker and darker, the four friends huddled together, wondering in silence what was to happen next, and if they'd ever get home.

Finally, the fourth day of their captivity came. Moses was ready for his mission across town with Matt. The old man now wore a clean white shirt and a brown wool jacket. His long gray hair was tied back with a black ribbon. He carried a large leather bag over his shoulder and a black felt tricorn hat in his hands.

"It is time we left," he told Matt. "You're to stay by my side at all times and do as I say if you want to be reunited with your sister and your friends."

Matt swallowed hard. He'd been anxiously

waiting for this moment. But now that it had arrived, the thought of going off with the old spy into enemy territory suddenly filled him with dread.

"Hurry, we've no time to waste," Moses said gruffly. "Travel through the city has become most dangerous. The King's soldiers are everywhere, looking to rout out Patriots. From here on in, I am Master Hastings, a Latin teacher, running a school for orphans. And you, young Matthew Carlton, are my prized student. From now on, you will address me only as Master Hastings. Understood?"

"Understood," Matt answered.

Moses turned to Hooter, Q, and Tony. "You three will remain in the mill until we return."

As Moses stepped outside to talk with his men, the four friends huddled together to say their good-byes.

"Watch out for the redcoats," Hooter warned. "And don't get hit by a musket ball."

"Actually," Q said matter-of-factly, "most deaths during the Revolution were not caused by musket balls but by infection."

"Is that supposed to make me feel better?" Matt asked.

"Don't worry, chief," said Tony. "We're not going anywhere. We'll be here when you get back."

Matt felt a lump in his throat. "You guys are the best, and whatever happens," he whispered, "we're all going home together."

"Together!" they cried. "Together!"

Without another word, Matt followed Moses out of the mill and down the narrow frozen road.

A short while later, the bare branches of the arching oaks and sturdy maples glistened in the stark afternoon light. The air was raw and biting cold. Matt kept a constant lookout over the open fields for Katie and the girls. As the mill disappeared into the distance, Matt grew more and more anxious. He was not at all sure he could be as brave as Moses needed him to be.

A rabbit rustled through the brush beside them. Matt suddenly jumped at the loud *rat-a-tat-tat* that punctured the quiet.

"It is only a woodpecker," the old man assured him. "Look up there in that hemlock tree."

Matt looked up to see a redheaded bird pecking on the bark of the evergreen.

"Ever make a bow and arrow from the wood of a hemlock?" Moses asked.

Matt shook his head no.

"Or a whistle from the wood of a chestnut?" The old man pointed to another tree.

"I don't really know much about wood or trees," Matt admitted.

Moses's eyebrow arched. "How is it you come from the west and do not know trees?"

"We don't spend much time outdoors, the way you do here," Matt told him. He thought about all the time he and his friends spent inside, watching TV or playing video games or being driven to the mall.

Moses nodded. "Ah, I've heard the Indian tribes are fierce in the western parts. 'Tis a shame. My brother and I always loved the woods."

"What about your sister? Did she follow you into the woods, too? My little sister, Katie, is always following me around and getting into trouble. It's because of her that we're lost out here now." Matt became quiet at the thought of Katie.

But the old man frowned. "I said I *had* a sister. She is dead to me now."

"I'm sorry," Matt said. "How did she die?"

"She married a Tory. That is how. And from the moment she vowed to love the Crown as well as her husband, she ceased to be my sister," Moses said grimly.

"At least you've still got Harry," Matt said.

The old man's face softened, and he smiled a

wistful smile. "He was quite the rascal in our child-
hood, but today, there is no man I could call a better
friend than my brother, Harry. His heart is as big as
his smile. You will see how special he is."

"What do you mean?" Matt asked.

"We are meeting him in the city," Moses told
him. "That big coat you are wearing is for him."

Matt fingered the wooden buttons on the coat.
"Is your brother a Patriot, like you?"

"Oh, aye, and he took to soldiering like a duck
to water. He loved to play the warrior as a boy. He'd
wield his little wooden sword and call himself Harry
the Brave. Now he carries a musket and fights redcoats. And like me, he would send all of them
packing back to England, if he could.

"Think of it, Matthew, a country without the
tyranny of a king, where every man is free to make
his own destiny." His voice suddenly sounded so
energetic and youthful, Matt almost forgot what an
old man he was. "Can you imagine living in such a
land, lad?"

Matt smiled to himself. "Definitely," he said.

Moses laughed. "Well, my young friend, it seems
you've the vision of a Patriot and the spunk of a spy.
I knew I had the right boy for the job the moment I
laid eyes on you. Matthew. That's a good strong name
you've got there. With Harry the Brave joining us,

I'll wager we three could set the world right, aye? Look out, King George! Here we come!"

The two walked on in silence, but Matt could hardly contain his excitement. He was no longer just an ordinary fifth-grade boy from Essex Elementary School in Rumson, Nebraska. He was Matthew Carlton, a Patriot spy about to meet a brave warrior! About to set the world right! Look out, King George, look out!

SIXTEEN

Traitors

As the two walked side by side, the land-scape gave way to narrow cobblestone streets lined with weathered houses, brick shops, and wooden fish stalls. The people who passed them on the footpaths and the shopkeepers who stood in front of their wares all seemed grim-faced and wary. The air was full of mistrust.

"My brother will be meeting us in front of the apothecary shop," Moses said, leading the way up a hill.

Matt was eager to meet Harry the Brave. But when three soldiers in red coats and black hats suddenly appeared, Matt grabbed hold of the old man's sleeve.

"Keep your eyes lowered, and let me do the talking," Moses whispered as the soldiers approached.

"Good day to you, sir," one of the soldiers said.

Moses didn't flinch but returned a confident nod.

"Your grandson?" the soldier asked, nodding to Matt.

"My student," Moses corrected him.

Matt held his breath and stared down at his feet. He stole a look at Moses, whose face remained a mask of calm. The sentry looked as if he wanted to question them further, but his attention turned to a pretty girl who was passing by. When the hem of her skirt suddenly caught on the nail of a barrel beside a cooper's shop, the soldier sprang to her rescue.

Weak with relief, Matt once again followed closely behind Moses. Geese waddled over the cobblestone street, and Moses pushed Matt aside as a house-maid emptied the contents of a chamber pot from a second-story window. Afterward, men in white wigs, long coats, and silver-buckled shoes dodged the spots of newly-colored snow.

As they walked on, Matt was struck by the strange, eerie stillness and quiet of the streets that lacked the sounds of car and truck engines.

"Stay close," Moses cautioned again as they approached a small crowd gathered before the apoth-ecary shop. The shop's door was boarded over like many of the other stores on the street. The large glass jars and assorted vials in the window were empty and covered in dust. Many Patriots had left the city, abandoning their homes and businesses.

They waited anxiously as the restless crowd grew larger. A baby cried in her mother's arms. Matt looked down the street. Everyone was straining to see what was happening.

"They're coming! They're coming!" a boy hollered down from the lamppost he had climbed.

"I want to see the faces of those lobsterbacks so I can spit on them," shouted a man who stood close by.

The loud syncopated slap of leather on stone suddenly rang out in the chill morning air. Matt felt every muscle in his body tighten. What was happening? The people in the crowd held their breath. And then he saw them: the bloodred jackets and high black boots on the well-drilled soldiers marching in step down the middle of the street. People pushed onto the footpaths to get out of their way.

"Murderers!" someone taunted from the crowd.

"Blasted bloodybacks, go back home!" another hollered.

But if they hoped to get a rise out of the soldiers, they were to be disappointed. The men's chiseled faces above the trim red coats showed no emotion. Their eyes peered neither to the left nor the right but were locked forward.

It was the loud rumble of a wagon's wheels that brought the crowd to a deadly silence. Matt leaned forward to look and was horrified by what he saw. For the wagon was rigged with a wooden frame. Hanging from the bar atop the frame were three large butcher's hooks that held the dead bodies of three young men! From each of their necks hung a sign painted in bold red letters that said TRAITOR!

Matt felt sick to his stomach at the horrible sight. The crowd gasped. An old woman clicked her tongue. "Look at the one in the middle," she said, pointing a gnarled finger. "Even all bloodied, you can see what a handsome lad he must have been. 'Tis a crime to see such a fair face end up on the end of a meat hook."

"Fair or ugly, the Crown would see all Patriot faces rot the same in the ground," someone else shouted.

"King George has a heart as cold as a headstone," said another.

It was then that Matt felt Moses's trembling hand on his shoulder.

"What is it?" Matt asked, seeing the old man's face crumple. He followed Moses's gaze back to the body of the handsome young rebel in the wagon. "Do you know him?"

"Aye," Moses whispered. "I know him well. For he is" — his voice cracked as he struggled to get the words out — "my little brother." Moses hung his head. "Oh, Harry, what have they done to you?" he cried. "My God, what have they done?"

SEVENTEEN

Blood on His Cuff

MOSES CLUTCHED HIS CHEST AS IF HE'D BEEN stabbed in the heart. His wrinkled face contorted with grief. Matt stole another look at the lifeless body on the cart.

Was that really the brave and wonderful Harry? It was too horrible to imagine. No wonder Moses and Dr. Franklin wanted to rid the colonies of the King's men for good.

"What ails the old man?" someone asked.

"Does he know one of the dead Patriots?" asked another.

Matt led Moses away from the crowd and down a narrow, dark alley. The air was foul with the stink of stale rum and rotting garbage. But they were safe there, hidden in the shadows. Matt found two wooden crates. "You can rest here," he told Moses.

"I should have been with him. I should have protected my brother," Moses whispered hoarsely. He made a fist, the veins in his neck bulging as his voice rose in anger. "But I promise you this, young Matthew. My brother will not have died in vain. I'll see those bloodthirsty redcoats rooted out of our colonies once and for all. It's what Harry fought for and what he died for. And I've nothing but this ache in my gut and hole in my heart to steer me now." His voice cracked once more.

He didn't speak for a long time after that. Together the two went back out to the street, where they found people going about their usual business. There were no signs of the soldiers or the wagon anywhere. They walked four long blocks in silence before they heard the call of a bugle and the sound of marching feet.

Matt feared that it was the same ghastly procession again, but it turned out to be a small battalion of soldiers doing their daily drill. He was following Moses to a corner where a coach was parked when a soldier came up behind them.

"Keep walking. Do not look back," Moses whispered, walking away from the coach. "This way," he said, turning to the left. Matt did as he was told, but he could hear the soldier's footsteps following behind them.

"Turn here," Moses said, heading down a side street. But it wasn't a side street at all. It was an alley that dead-ended into a building!

"Lost your way, sir?" the soldier asked. His youthful voice echoed in the alley.

"Seems I have," the old man answered coolly.

The soldier casually laid his musket against the wall and then pulled a brass flask from his coat. Matt studied his round face and rosy-colored cheeks as the soldier took a drink. He couldn't have been more than seventeen or eighteen years old.

"Those are strange shoes and breeches you wear, lad," he said, wiping his mouth with the back of his hand.

"He is not from this colony," Moses quickly interjected.

"I just got here," Matt added.

He saw Moses blink, and in that blink he knew he'd said the wrong thing! Matt's eyes fell back on the soldier's musket and the sharpened steel of the bayonet that rested against the rough bricks.

"Just got here?" The soldier's eyebrow shot up. "From where?"

"From —" Moses began to answer, but the soldier cut him off.

"I asked the boy," he said.

"From . . . from the west," Matt sputtered.

"You recently traveled into the city with the harbor closed and the roads blocked?" The soldier eyed him suspiciously.

Matt's heart felt as if it would beat right out of his chest.

"Perhaps you'd like to follow me to our guardhouse and explain to my captain just how you managed that miracle," the soldier said, reaching for his musket.

But as he did, Moses lunged forward, and the soldier jabbed him hard in the side with his bayonet. The two wrestled to the ground. Matt grabbed the soldier's musket. It was heavy in his hands. Moses slammed the soldier against the wall. He hit it with a loud thud. As the young soldier slumped to the ground and went limp, Moses took the musket out of Matt's hands.

"Get out of here! Now!" he ordered in a breathless voice.

"B-but," Matt stammered.

"Wait for me in the street. Go now!" Moses shouted.

Matt raced to the end of the alley, his heart pounding with every step.

A few moments later, Moses joined him in the street. His steely gaze invited no questions. But when he caught Matt staring at the blood on his cuff and seeping through his jacket, he frowned. "Give me your coat, now!" he ordered.

"Is he dead?" Matt whispered as he slipped out of the big coat and handed it over.

Moses nodded. His face was white as ash and his hands were trembling. "He was hardly old enough to grow a beard."

Matt swallowed hard. "Then why did you have to kill him?"

Moses frowned. "If I had let him live we would both have been swinging by the hangman's noose by noon tomorrow. This war is madness . . ." Moses said, his voice trailing off. "And no one is spared — not him, nor my Harry, no one. . . ."

Just then another soldier appeared in the distance.

"Now run, boy! Run!" Moses ordered.

Matt ran as fast as he could. He looked back once to see Moses disappear around a corner, with the soldier on his heels. Matt crossed a street. He was running so fast, he ran straight into the same trio of redcoats they had seen earlier!

"What's your hurry, lad?" one of them growled, grabbing Matt's arm.

"Where are you running to, then?" another soldier demanded.

Matt's head was suddenly swimming. He had to say something quick. The soldier tightened his grip.

"I was just playing with my friends," Matt managed to lie. "Did you see which way they went?"

"Playing with your friends?" asked the soldier, giving Matt a hard shake. "Well, watch your step, boy, for you wouldn't want to run into the end of my saber, would you?" The other soldiers laughed.

The three continued down the street. Matt shrank back against the building in a cold sweat. Harry was dead. Moses was gone. And the redcoats were everywhere!

What will I do now? Matt thought. *What am I going to do?*

EIGHTEEN

Topsy-Turvy

DAYS PASSED IN THE HEWSON HOUSEHOLD, and the mood had turned as gray as the ash in the bucket beside the hearth. Little Patience continued to burn with fever. Her mother refused to leave her side. The servants whispered among themselves at their worry that the pox had descended upon the house. And all the doctor could say was "only time will tell."

Meanwhile, the sky over Boston filled with snow clouds, and the house on Milk Street grew dark and drafty. Wood was in short supply in the city, and even the wealthy could no longer afford to have a fire in every room.

Katie and the twins sat before the sewing room hearth, where the Hewson girls worked on their embroidery samplers. As the distant boom of cannon fire sounded from outside the windows, Master

Hewson was quick to assure everyone that there was nothing to worry about.

"General Howe and the King's men are keeping the city safe from the rebels," he told them. "Our colonies will soon be restored to order under His Majesty's law."

"He doesn't have a clue about what's going to happen," Lily whispered as the three spoke quietly among themselves.

"I wish we could go home," Emma whispered back glumly.

"Can't we just leave now and go look for Matt?" Katie whispered.

"You heard what Mistress Hewson said. The streets are too dangerous. And when we do leave, you'll have to be able to run. You can barely stand now," Lily reminded her.

Katie looked down at her ankle, which was blue and swollen, with a nasty, oozing cut running across the top. She still cried out in pain every time she took a step. No, they weren't going anywhere for a while.

To pass the time, the Hewson sisters taught Katie and the twins to sing songs in rounds and to play Mr. Red Cap, Cat and Mouse, and other fun games. They even made a game of trading hair ribbons. Katie tore a bright yellow bow off her dress and traded it for one of Charity's blue velvet hair ribbons, which she wore as a headband to hold back her curls. They told one another their favorite stories and roasted chestnuts on the hearth.

"Katie, would you like to help me work on my sampler?" asked Charity.

"I've never used a needle and thread before," Katie told her.

"A girl of seven years, and you don't know how to sew!" Faith exclaimed.

"'Tis most unfortunate," added Hope, clicking her tongue. "She shall never find a husband."

"You needn't worry, Katie," Charity assured her. "For I shall teach you everything I know."

While Charity taught Katie how to thread a needle, Lily taught Mercy a secret handshake that she and her friends had made up back home.

"You lock pinkies and touch thumbs," Lily said, demonstrating. "And you can only use it with your very best friends."

Mercy smiled as they locked pinkies and touched thumbs. "Best of friends?" she whispered.

"Best of friends," Lily whispered back.

The other girls resumed their storytelling and singing. But no matter how many songs they sang or how cozy the fire felt, they had only to move a few feet away from it to feel the pockets of chill in the cold, darkened house. The sound of cannon fire grew louder each day. At night the fear of the pox swirled through their dreams. And of all their fears and worries, the same one always stood out above the rest. How would they ever get back home?

One day, Mercy entered the sewing room with the baby in her arms, wrapped in a woolen shawl. "Papa has sent for the doctor again," she said gravely. "The doctor now feels sure that Patience has the pox."

"Mercy," Charity asked, "will Patience die?"

"Cook says that if you think it, it will be so," Faith told her.

"I can't stop thinking it," Charity said, bursting into tears.

"Papa!" Mercy cried, seeing her father in the doorway.

"What news of Patience?" Faith asked as she and her sisters gathered around him.

"Will she ever get better?" asked Hope.

Her father's eyes welled with tears. "God willing," he said. "Dr. Brenner is with her now." Then he paused and turned to Katie. "And I think it wise to let him see your ankle while he is here."

"Will he give me a shot?" Katie asked. "I hate shots."

Lily pinched Katie hard. "Shots haven't been invented yet," she whispered sharply into Katie's ear.

"No need to be frightened," Master Hewson said to Katie. "You must think of us as your safe harbor while you are here in the colonies." His words wrapped around the girls like a hug. But he was the enemy. How could someone be so kind and also be your enemy?

Master Hewson slipped the small wooden penny-whistle from his vest pocket and brought it to his lips. They all grew quiet as the soft, gentle notes of their favorite lullaby filled the room. Even the baby stopped fussing and cooed.

Katie and the twins joined the Hewson girls as they sang sweetly in their favorite round.

Lavender's blue, diddle diddle,
Lavender's green,
When I am king, diddle diddle,
You shall be queen.

For a few precious moments, all of their cares and worries over fevers and mobs, shortages and soldiers, were swept away by a song.

"Papa," Hope said when the song was over. "Is it true that if General Washington took over the city, we'd not be able to sing 'Rule Britannia' anymore?"

"Why, I would challenge any man to a duel who'd dare to stop me and my pennywhistle from playing a tune for my girls. Thankfully, we still have King George's soldiers here in the city. I have total faith they will keep that scoundrel Washington and his rebel hotheads at bay."

"Cook says that Patsy Reynolds's mother is spinning flax for the rebel soldiers and that her father will not allow them to brew English tea," Faith announced.

"I think it horrid that they are so disloyal to our King," Hope declared.

Lily wished she could tell them that staying loyal to King George was the wrong thing to do. If only she could tell them that the King was going to lose the war. If only she could tell them that they were on the wrong side!

"One always must stand by one's own convictions," Master Hewson said.

"But how do you know that you are right?" Lily asked.

There was a sad weariness in Master Hewson's

eyes that Lily hadn't seen before. But his voice was gentle as ever.

"To be honest with you, there was once a time I thought I knew all of the answers," he said with a half smile. "But now I don't know. Everything feels so — topsy-turvy. So many are clamoring for change."

"But isn't change a good thing?" Lily persisted.

"Loyalty and obedience are God's way," Master Hewson said. "Rebelliousness is the way of the devil. We must remain true to our king — and be thankful for all God has blessed us with."

"But some people in the colonies are starving. Wouldn't change be better for them?" asked Lily.

Master Hewson sighed. "In the end, I find I can only be true to my beliefs. I have to provide for my family — as my love for them is what guides me."

Lily's heart sank. How would she ever be able to change his mind in time?

"Papa, will you play us 'Lavender's Blue' again?" Faith begged.

"No! Play 'The Nightingale,'" pleaded Charity.

"When I return from looking in on Patience," he promised, "I shall play you all the tunes you wish — for a fee of hugs and kisses, of course." With a wink he blew a few notes on his whistle, and his girls covered him with kisses.

Once he had left the room, Lily looked anxiously at her twin. Their hosts were loyal to a king who wanted to squash General Washington and the rebellion. There was pox in the house, a disease that could spread and kill everyone. And all Master Hewson could do was play songs on his pennywhistle! Their safe harbor didn't feel very safe at all.

A short while later, as the girls continued their games, they heard a bloodcurdling scream.

"They've begun to bleed Patience," Mercy said.

Lily's face went white. "*Bleed* her?"

"Yes, to rid her body of any ill humors," Faith explained.

"The doctor has brought a big bottle full of leeches that he will use to suck out her blood," Mercy added. "And he thinks Katie should be bled as well."

"Katie?" Lily and Emma cried together.

"Of course," Mercy nodded. "He says the leeches will do the wound on her ankle a world of good."

NINETEEN

Trust No One

MATT'S HEART FELT AS IF IT WOULD LEAP OUT of his chest when Moses returned from the alley.

"We've *got* to get out of here!" Moses struggled to speak as he doubled over in pain.

Matt could tell that Moses's wound had worsened.

"I just need to rest here a moment," Moses said, sinking down onto a step. He dropped his head back and closed his eyes. His face was ghostly white.

Matt stared at Moses as his chest rose and fell. And he panicked when he realized that the old man might die right then and there.

"We have to get to Bell's Tavern *now*," Moses wheezed, struggling to his feet with a grimace. "I had hoped to walk, but that's impossible. We'll need to get a coach."

They reached the tavern just as a boy was lighting the coach's lamps to ready it for departure. The sun was sinking fast behind a tall brick bell tower. The coach was full as Matt and Moses squeezed in. It had eight passengers, four to a seat, and one smelly, wet dog that lay on the floor by their feet.

The ride across town was slow and bumpy. Moses sat mute, his face drained of color and grim with pain.

Matt looked out the window as they bumped along the narrow cobblestone streets. He had a sinking feeling that he was going farther and farther away from everyone he knew and would never see them again. A sharp wind rattled the coach doors and windows and whistled its way into the cab. The stink from the dog and the moldy straw on the cab's floor was overpowering.

When one of the passengers asked Moses his occupation, the old man quickly pulled himself together and mentioned the school he planned to open for orphans in the city.

Matt marveled at the calm with which Moses lied. There was no hint of pain or hesitation catching his voice. There couldn't be, for their lives depended upon it.

The dog began to bark hysterically as the coach lurched to a sudden stop. From the window, Matt watched redcoats on horseback surrounding the coach. He shrank back at the sight of a young British officer on his horse, just inches away from him! The soldier's brass buckles and buttons gleamed against his brushed red coat. He rode so close to them, Matt could almost have reached out and touched him.

"What the devil do these redcoats want with us?" a passenger grumbled, reaching for his pistol beneath his greatcoat.

"Nay, show them no arms," Moses warned. "They do not mean to overtake us."

"How can you be so certain?" the passenger asked.

"They would have done it by now. They only mean to get around us," Moses said. His eyes darted from one window to the other. And no sooner had he said it than the soldiers rode out in front of the coach and disappeared down a hill.

Matt sank back into his seat, his heart once again racing. He sat on his hands to keep them from trembling.

"Too bad — I would have enjoyed putting a bullet into one of His Majesty's men," the passenger muttered, tucking his pistol back under his coat.

Moses said nothing. He closed his eyes until the coach finally came to a stop. Three passengers departed; two new passengers came aboard. The coachman cracked his bull-hide whip, and the horses broke into a canter. As the coach lurched along,

Matt noticed a dark mole on the new passenger's hand beside him. It was an odd-looking mole, in the shape of a perfect little bell.

The coach swerved sharply to the right, and the man's leather bag fell open. Papers scattered all over the floor, mostly charcoal drawings of landscapes. The man and his friend beside him rushed to pick them up.

Matt reached down to help. He picked up a sketch of a crossroads and a bridge.

"Hey, ho! What are you about?" one of the men shouted, pulling the paper so violently from Matt's hands that it ripped in two.

"I was just trying to help," Matt said. But the passenger scowled with an anxious look in his eyes.

"Do you draw for your pleasure, young sir?" another passenger asked. But the other young man was quick to answer for his friend.

"Nay, sir, he draws for coin. My comrade and I are surveyors." He smiled a tight smile and turned to look at Matt. "So, lad, are you traveling on your own?"

Matt hesitated. "I am with my teacher, Master Hastings," he lied. He stole a look at Moses, but the old spy's face remained unmoved.

"What school in the city do you attend?" the man persisted.

"'Tis a new school for orphans," Moses quickly answered for him.

Matt could feel the man looking him over. "Those are most unusual shoes you wear, boy," he noted. "What shoemaker cobbled such strange creations?"

Matt's eyes darted to his sneakers. "M-my mother bought them for me."

"I thought you said your school was for orphans," the man said, giving Moses a suspicious look.

Once again, Matt's heart raced so fast he thought it would burst, when he realized the blunder he had made. "I — I —" he stuttered.

"He is newly orphaned," Moses quickly intervened. "Tragic loss. Both parents taken in a fire. The memories are still fresh."

This lie, told so swiftly, so smoothly, instantly silenced the man. But as Matt looked at Moses, he saw a red stain coming through the side of his coat!

"Whoa!" the coachman suddenly shouted, pulling on the reins and bringing the coach to an abrupt halt. The passengers turned their attention to gathering up their belongings. Matt caught Moses's gaze and nodded to the stain on his coat. Moses quickly covered it with his bag.

"Bell's Tavern," the coachman called. He opened the cab door. "And for those of you journeying on, we'll be stopping here to water the horses. The inn-keeper's wife bakes a fine pigeon pie, and the house ale is hearty."

The dark-haired surveyor turned to Matt. "Well, lad, here is where we part ways. Have a care as you travel through the city."

"Aye, with the redcoats in town, there's no telling where you'll run into a brigade," his friend added. "And here is a guinea toward some books for that new school of yours." He placed a coin in Matt's hands.

"They were friendly enough," Matt said as the surveyors headed for the tavern.

Moses took the coin from his hand. "They are English and probably spies," he said, following the two men's every step with his eyes.

"Spies!" Matt exclaimed. "But they warned us against the redcoats. And they said they were surveyors."

"And I said you were an orphan," Moses reminded him. "In these times you can trust no one. I would stake my life that those two are English gentry. Their accents and their clean boots give them away."

"But they seemed so nice," Matt said.

"Nice enough to sketch every crossroads and bridge from Boston to Concord on General Howe's orders, I'll wager," Moses said with a groan. "And nice enough to hand us over to a firing squad should they learn what we are about."

He grabbed Matt's arm with one hand, his fingernails digging through Matt's shirt. "This is no game we play at, Matthew. There is nothing *nice* about war. It feeds on lies and treachery. It is about killing or being killed. You saw what they did to my brother. Unless you want the same thing to happen to you, trust no one. Do you hear me? Trust no one."

TWENTY

A Brother Comes to Call

Silently, Matt followed behind Moses, his eyes darting about watching for any movement, his ears pricking up at the slightest sound. With one of their soldiers dead, surely the redcoats must be hunting throughout the city for his killer. Matt couldn't stop the nightmare that was forming in his mind. He pictured himself on a cart beside Moses, their lifeless bodies hanging from meat hooks with signs saying TRAITOR! dangling from their necks!

"Can't we go back to the mill now?" Matt pleaded as Moses moaned and bent over in agony. "Wouldn't it be safer for you to rest there?"

"We've a mission to accomplish now," Moses told him. His voice was so weak, Matt hardly recognized it. "We cannot return until we do. But I know someone who lives close by."

They turned down a quiet street lined with houses, and Moses leaned on Matt's shoulder as he walked. Most of the windows were dark or shuttered tight. Moses moved slowly, groaning now with every step.

"It's that brick house across the street," he panted. He slowed to a stop and grabbed on to a hitching post. "I just . . . just need to rest."

"Here, lean on me," Matt told him. "I'll help you."

They managed to get across the street and up the brick steps to the house's front door. Moses pointed to the brass door knocker, and Matt reached up and rapped it against the door. Moments later, a young servant boy appeared.

"Can I help you, sir?" he asked, straightening the wig that sat crooked on his head.

"Tell your mistress that her brother has come to call," Moses said, struggling to get the words out.

The boy stared at Moses, then backed up and disappeared for a long while.

"You're to follow me," he said when he finally returned, and he led the way up three flights of stairs. Matt followed behind, with Moses leaning heavily on his arm. Once they had reached an attic bedroom, Moses sank down onto a bed in a corner of the room.

"I'll be back with some wood to make up your fire," the young servant told them, setting a candle on the table and hurrying out the door.

Then, to Matt's amazement, he saw Moses pull off his long beard and remove his hat and the gray wig under it — to reveal a head of thick blond hair! He looked very much like his brother, Harry.

"The wrinkles have been put on with paste," Moses admitted. "Disguise is part and parcel of the shady business I am in."

Matt stared in stunned silence as Moses peeled away his mask.

"You're not really an old man!" exclaimed Matt.

"Old enough at five and twenty to have seen more blood spilled in the name of the Crown than I can stomach," the young spy said.

"And your name? Is it really Moses?"

"Nay. God's not seen fit to come down from his heaven with tablets to guide me through this miserable world of ours. For I am only a Thomas, Thomas Jamison. Not a Moses at all."

As Matt looked at Thomas's face in the candlelight, he saw that the young spy's eyes had closed and rivulets of sweat covered his forehead. Even more frightening, the bed's white quilt was now stained red with his blood!

The door opened slowly, and a woman in a long satin dress and a tall white wig appeared. "Thomas, why have you come?" she asked stiffly.

Thomas opened his eyes. "Martha, I know it has been too long —" he began.

"Too long?" she bristled. "Too long? Your nieces still do not understand why you've not visited them these twelve months past. Did you even know you had a nephew, born last summer?"

"I did not know," Thomas admitted.

"No, how could you?" she said, her lip trembling. "Because you and Harry are like strangers to me now."

Thomas let out a sad sigh. "Martha, what divides us —"

"Will always divide us," she cut him off. "For my loyalties must be with my husband and my King."

"I — I — need your help," he panted. It was then that she stepped inside and saw the blood on the blanket.

"Oh, Thomas, you are hurt!" she cried, flying to his side.

He struggled to speak. "It is only a scratch compared to what they did to our Harry."

His sister clutched the white lace shawl that was knotted at her chest. "What about Harry?" she whispered. "Tell me, brother, what has happened to our Harry?"

But Thomas's head dropped to his chest as he lost consciousness.

"Wait here with him," the woman ordered Matt. "Dr. Brenner is still in the house. I will fetch him straightaway."

She hurried out of the room and quickly returned with the doctor at her side. He went directly to Thomas, and after several minutes he shot Matt a suspicious look. "How did he come by this wound?" the doctor demanded.

"'Twas an accident," Thomas's sister told him before Matt could answer.

"An accident, you say?" the doctor repeated with a suspicious glint in his eye. "I will need water and bandages."

The woman rushed back out of the room.

"Now tell me the truth, boy," the doctor said, turning to Matt. "Did this accident have something to do with a British soldier's bayonet?"

Matt hesitated, not knowing how to answer. "There was a fight," he said finally. The doctor shook his head and continued his work.

Thomas's sister returned to the room with a basin of water and some strips of cloth. "Will he live?" she asked anxiously.

"'Twill be a miracle," the doctor said. "He appears to have lost a great deal of blood."

"God help him," the woman murmured. "Will you return in the morning to check on him and my daughter?"

The doctor's face clouded. "I'm afraid, Mistress Hewson, I can no longer offer you my services. You can try fetching old Mistress Coup. She has a house near Oliver's dock."

"But she is no doctor!" Mistress Hewson exclaimed.

Doctor Brenner shrugged. "The old woman keeps leeches and can probably be persuaded to continue your daughter's bleeding in return for some meat or flour."

"But you *must* come back!" begged Mistress Hewson.

" 'Tis only my friendship for you and your family that keeps me from reporting this matter to the guards," the doctor told her. "Your brother's loyalties are well known in this city. If you know what is good for you, you'll get him out of your house as soon as you can." With that, he closed his bag briskly and hurried out the door.

The woman turned to Matt. He could see her dark eyes full of worry. "What did Thomas mean about something happening to our brother, Harry?" she asked. "If you know, I implore you to tell me."

Matt hesitated. How could he tell her of the ghastly sight he'd seen?

"Please," she begged, putting her hand on his. "Please tell me. Is he alive?"

Matt shook his head.

She clutched her chest and sank down onto the bed, as if she'd been struck in the heart. "Not Harry!" she moaned. "Not my little brother. Not Harry! Not Harry!"

Just then, another man walked into the room. He took one look at Thomas, who was still unconscious on the bed.

"Good Lord, what is he doing here?" the man exclaimed.

"Oh, husband, he is wounded," his wife told him. "And Harry is dead!" She broke down wailing as her husband took her into his arms.

"Harry was so young," she cried. "Not even twenty."

Her husband's face darkened. "Young, perhaps, but he made a choice."

"He was too young to choose," she cried, breaking free of him. She took a rag from the basin and gently washed the sweat from Thomas's forehead.

Meanwhile, her husband looked at Matt, as if suddenly noticing him for the first time. "And who might you be?"

"I'm Matthew Carlton," Matt told him.

"Does your mother know where you are, lad? And the dangerous business you are about?"

"No, sir," Matt said truthfully. "I didn't want to come here. I didn't even want to leave home," he blurted out. "I just need to find —"

"How old are you, son?" the man interrupted.

"I'm ten years old," answered Matt.

The man's kind face contorted with anger. "Enough!" he cried. "I've had enough of this madness. Our colonies are ripped apart. Our families divided. Young boys are sent on missions meant for men. For what? For tax on a cup of tea?"

His wife stroked Thomas's forehead and sobbed. "Oh, Thomas, what is to become of you?"

"He has to leave," her husband said, regaining his composure. "They must both leave."

"But he is wounded! And he is my brother!" his wife pleaded.

"He is a rebel and a traitor," her husband exploded once more. "If we harbor a traitor, they will hang us alongside of him. Think of our children, Martha. We cannot risk it. We dare not for their sake. 'Tis bad enough the doctor has seen him. God willing, he'll keep our secret."

"But, William —" she begged.

"You must leave this matter to me," he said, guiding her to the door. "Go now. We have enough to worry about with the pox in our home and our daughter so ill. Your place is with the children. Do not tell Mercy or the rest of the girls. No one is to know he is here. We will sort this out in the morning."

Once his wife had gone, the man turned back to Matt. "You're not to leave this room," he ordered. He took a wrought-iron key from a hook on the wall. "I am locking you in. No one is to know you are even in this house. Do you understand? Not a soul is to know you are here."

TWENTY-ONE

Wolf Hunter

"THOMAS, PLEASE WAKE UP," MATT BEGGED as he leaned over the unconscious young rebel.

But Thomas didn't stir. As he studied the rebel's face, Matt was startled to see how young Thomas looked without his makeup. "They think you and the others are criminals," Matt continued. "And your sister and her husband called you a traitor! Why don't they understand?"

Matt sank down to his knees and put his head next to Thomas. "Please stay alive," he whispered. "*Please, please, please* stay alive."

Matt awoke the next morning and wondered if it had all been a dream. He rubbed his eyes, hoping to find himself in his own bed, back home in Nebraska. But he quickly discovered that rather than his warm, comfy bed, he was lying on cold floorboards, with a stiff, thin quilt over him. A few feet away, Thomas's brother-in-law was emptying the ash from the fireplace. Matt sat up and looked over at the bed. Thomas's eyes were open, but his face was contorted with pain.

"I never thought I'd see the day that the gentry of Boston tend to their own fires," Thomas said sarcastically.

"I dare not risk my servants knowing any more of your visit here," his brother-in-law replied. There was a short silence. "I was sorry to hear about Harry," Master Hewson added, his voice softening.

"Will you see that he gets a proper burial, William?" Thomas whispered.

"I will do what I can," his brother-in-law replied. "It has never been my wish to see your sister and her family so divided. We are only following our conscience and what we believe is best for the colonies."

"Best for the Crown, you mean," Thomas replied.

"I was born and raised in this colony, Thomas. We Hewsons were among the earliest settlers in Massachusetts. All I've worked for is here." Master Hewson's voice rose with emotion. "I'll not see it all torn down for some half-baked scheme that Sam Adams and a group of lawless ruffians in Philadelphia have concocted." A tense silence followed.

"I am sorry that I cannot offer you the safety of our home."

"Will you turn your wife's only living brother over to the hangman, then?" Thomas shot back.

Matt held his breath as he looked from one man to the next.

But Master Hewson shook his head. "You are still family, Thomas. Your politics cannot change the love your sister feels for you. I am well acquainted with a carpenter who has turned his hands from cabinetry to coffins of late. Business is booming, and fear of the fever is now so great that the coffin-maker's wagon has been one of the few they'll pass on through with little inspection. I will arrange for you and the boy to leave here, hidden in two of his coffins."

"Has this carpenter pledged for the colonies?" asked Thomas.

"Nay. The man does not take sides, but he will take gold."

"Can he get us safely across the city?" Thomas asked.

"I will see if today is possible," Master Hewson told him.

Matt grew hopeful. He even let himself hope that the girls might turn up at the mill.

"Can you at least give me until tonight to regain my strength for the journey?" Thomas pleaded. "I beg of you, William."

Master Hewson hesitated.

"Just until tonight, so my sister does not have to bury a second brother in the same week," Thomas said convincingly.

"As you wish," Master Hewson relented. "But you must not stay a moment longer. Tonight at midnight you must both be gone."

"I shall not forget this kindness," Thomas said, closing his eyes.

"Rest now, while you can," his brother-in-law told him.

But no sooner had Master Hewson left the room than Thomas's eyes flew open. "Come closer, Matthew," he called. "I must count on you now."

Matt moved closer to the bed.

"There is no time to waste," Thomas whispered. "One of General Washington's spies is wearing an English officer's uniform and has important information that the General needs. There is also intelligence that the General hopes to put into the redcoats' hands to lead them astray. Harry was meant to make the exchange. And alas, I am too weak. So now you must do it instead."

"Me!" Matt squeaked. "But I don't know anything about being a spy."

"On the contrary, my young friend," Thomas said. "You've already been quite successful at it."

"What do you mean?"

"You've already carried one message into the city in that big coat you wore," Thomas told him. "Fetch it for me, please."

Matt took the coat from the chair and handed it to Thomas. Thomas turned over one of the large wooden buttons. And as he gave it a push, it slid open to reveal a false bottom with a tiny rolled piece of paper inside it.

"What does it say?" Matt asked.

"It is written in Dr. Franklin's invisible stain," Thomas said. "It's best you not know the contents. But know this: If that message gets into the wrong hands, General Washington and his army would be in grave danger, and you might not live to see your next birthday," he said ominously.

Matt gulped. "Where do I have to go?" he asked.

"A house not far from here. You can walk. There is to be a ball there tonight," Thomas told him. "A man dressed in a British officer's uniform will be waiting to make the exchange."

"Is that why you asked for more time?"

Thomas nodded. "I'm sorry I had to lie, but I could not very well tell him the truth. My brother-in-law is a goodhearted man and easily persuaded. I'm afraid this war calls for men made of stronger stuff than he."

"But he is risking his life for you," Matt protested. "And he is your family."

Matt was confused. Master Hewson was a Loyalist and the enemy. But he had a good heart. Shouldn't the enemy be bad? If some were good and some were bad, how could anyone know who to fight in a war?

"You'll find the house easily enough," Thomas said, cutting into Matt's thoughts. " 'Twill be the only house on the street lit up like daylight. And the place will be crawling with British officers." He paused to take a breath. "They'll need extra waiters to serve the punch. The house butler is warm to our cause and warmer still to the coin we will pay him. The password you're to give him is 'Wolf Hunter.' "

"But we're locked in," Matt reminded him.

Thomas smiled weakly. "My brother-in-law forgets that I grew up in this house and am intimate with every inch of the place. Go to the chimney and look for a chipped brick on the right side above the floor. Lift it out. There should be an extra key behind it. Once out in the hall, take the little stairway to the left. It leads down to the pantry, and from there you can slip out the back door without being seen." He laid his head back on the pillow and closed his eyes.

"What do you think will happen to your sister's family when the Patriots win the war? I — I mean, if they win the war," Matt said.

Thomas scowled. "Should we win this conflict, those who favor the Crown would do better to leave these colonies for good. They will not be welcome here."

"Then your sister and her family would have to leave," Matt pointed out. "They are your family. Won't you miss them? Besides, they were born here, and it's not fair to make them leave."

"War is not always fair. But if we do not take action, we risk losing everything," Thomas told him. "Do you not see that our very lives are governed by the King's whims? He is a tyrant. There is no fairness here. He taxes every penny we make. His soldiers loot our houses and tear down our fencing for firewood. He has closed our harbor and patrolled the roads leading in and out of the city. We've run out of meat and milk. Our people are starving. It is our very lives we fight for, and for the right to live decently." His eyes grew cold, and his voice fell to a whisper. "And what his men did to my brother, Harry, is a wrong I shall never forgive."

Matt thought of Katie and how hard it was to be apart, not knowing if she was safe. How would he feel if his home was being looted and his family threatened? He had to help the Patriots. He had to help Thomas complete the mission.

He walked over to the hearth and searched for the broken brick. He gave it a tug and quickly found the black iron key.

"Good," Thomas whispered weakly. "But the hour grows late. You must make haste." Using his teeth and all of his strength, he tore the button from his coat and handed it over to Matt. "Put it in your pocket and keep it safe," he said.

"Once you leave this house, go around to the front and turn right. Then make your way down the street straightaway and keep walking until you come to the house ablaze with light and with many carriages waiting out front. You're to go to the side door, where a butler will let you in. Tell him Moses sent you. Give him this." He took a gold coin from his vest pocket.

"What should I do once I get inside?" Matt asked, slipping the coin safely into his pocket next to the button.

"The butler will instruct you," Thomas told him. "He'll have a footman's uniform for you to wear. Just remember to keep the button on you at all times. And don't draw attention to yourself. You'll be given a tray from which to serve punch to the guests. You must look for a tall officer with a scar under his eye and the fourth button missing from the sleeve of his coat. Wait until he is alone. Then approach him. Make mention of his missing button. Listen closely for his reply. If he scolds you for speaking so brazenly, you either have the wrong man or the timing is too dangerous to make the transfer. Move away quickly."

Matt nodded, but his head was swimming with questions. What if he made a mistake? What if he dropped the tray? But there was no time for doubts. He had to pay attention. His life would depend upon it.

"You will know it is the right man if he answers with a nod and says these words: 'I did misplace my button and would be glad for another,'" Thomas continued. "Then you must take the button from your pocket. Do not hand it to him but rather place it on your tray next to his glass. He will take it and replace it with another. Put that button into your pocket and draw no attention to yourself."

"What should I do once I have the button?" Matt asked.

"Guard it with your life. For if it was to get into the wrong hands it would be your death warrant," Thomas told him. "And 'twould put all we struggle for in great jeopardy. Continue working until it is safe to leave by the door you came in. Whatever you do, you must get back here by midnight! Once outside, watch for the coffin-maker's wagon. God willing, we'll both be back at the mill by morning and —"

"But what about my sister?" Matt interrupted. "I need to find —"

"We mustn't be thinking of our own needs now." Thomas cut him off, his eyes flashing open. "General Washington and our countrymen are depending on us. What is at stake here is bigger than both of us. We have a chance to make a new country, to change the world, Matthew."

Thomas reached out and squeezed his wrist. "You are a good lad, and I'm sorry to have to draw one so young into such a dangerous endeavor. But you have my word, once we've got the information to General Washington, I'll do what I can to help you find your sister. We'll find her together. What do you say?"

"Together," Matt smiled.

"And when we do find her," Thomas continued with a wistful look in his eyes, "you must promise me something."

"What?" Matt asked.

"Don't ever lose her again," Thomas whispered hoarsely. "Too many families have been broken apart by this struggle already."

Matt knew he was talking about his own family and how divided they'd become. "I won't lose her again," Matt promised.

"You are a brave boy, Matthew," Thomas said, "and I am glad we got to meet."

"Me, too," Matt agreed.

"Promise me something else," he whispered, his green eyes pleading.

"Anything," Matt said.

"Promise me you'll stay alive," Thomas whispered weakly.

Matt nodded. "I'll try."

"Good. Now repeat the password," Thomas ordered.

"Wolf Hunter," Matt said softly. "Wolf Hunter."

TWENTY-TWO

So Much Fuss Over a Few Leeches!

AS THOMAS AND MATT WHISPERED THEIR plans in the Hewsons' attic, the Hewson girls led the twins and Katie down the hall to Patience's bedroom on the floor below.

"Now bite down! Bite down hard!" said Mistress Coup, the hefty old woman who stood beside the bed. Wisps of gray hair hung from her cap, and the hems of her skirts were stained and dirty. A bloodied rag hung over her arm, and in her wrinkled hands she held a large glass jar full of squirming, fat black leeches. She had placed a rope in Patience's mouth to bite down on to keep her from screaming.

Lily, Emma, and Katie looked on in horror from the doorway. Even more terrifying was the sight of little Patience lying on the bed — with her bare arms outstretched and five shiny black wormlike leeches sucking blood from the open vein in her arm!

"You can't do that to Katie!" cried Lily. Katie ran and hid behind the girls.

"It would be best if you all waited in the hall," said Master Hewson, hurrying them out of the room.

The twins pleaded with him to change his mind. He could not have Katie bled! It was only when the old woman came looking for Katie with her jar of hungry leeches in her hands that the twins turned around to find she had disappeared!

"Come now, child," barked Mistress Coup. "I haven't time for your nonsense."

But Katie was nowhere to be found.

Everyone joined in the search. Emma looked in the bedrooms on the second floor, while Lily went up to the attic on the third. There in the dark hallway she found a closed door. Lily jiggled the knob, but it was locked tight.

At the moment Lily was trying the doorknob, Matt was on the other side of the very same door. Quietly, he put the key into the lock. But he pulled back quickly as he heard the doorknob jiggle from the other side. Lily had given Matt such a fright, he almost fell over backward.

Not wanting to waste time with a locked door, Lily raced back downstairs, where she joined the

Hewson sisters as they searched the sewing room and the drawing room.

Meanwhile, Matt pressed his ear to the door and waited until he was sure the coast was clear. Then he put the key into the lock and slowly, soundlessly turned the knob. His heart beat wildly as he stole out into the hall and over to the back stairwell. But he stopped halfway down at the sudden pounding of footsteps and voices.

"We must look everywhere!" he heard Master Hewson order.

Matt panicked. Could Master Hewson have already discovered he'd gone? Would they turn him over to the redcoats if he caught him?

Matt sped down the stairs and tore out the back door before anyone could see him leave. He went so quickly, he forgot to close the door.

"Mama," called Charity, running up the stairs. "The back door is open!"

"Dear God, I hope she's not on the streets alone!" Mistress Hewson exclaimed.

"What about the room up on the third floor?" asked Lily. "The door was locked, but I think I heard something in there. Maybe Katie's locked herself in."

Mistress and Master Hewson exchanged panicked looks.

"That's impossible!" Master Hewson declared. "I am the only one with the key to that room. There is no way anyone could get in or out of there."

"We'd better try downstairs," Mistress Hewson suggested.

Suddenly, there came the sound of shattering glass below, followed by a scream. Master Hewson rushed down the stairs as Cook ran into the hall, wringing her hands.

"'Tis a mob, Master!" she cried. "'Tis a rebel mob!"

Master Hewson bolted the front door and secured the lock.

"What is going on?" Mistress Coup demanded.

"Yes, William, please tell us what has happened?" Mistress Hewson pleaded as the two looked down from the upstairs landing. Faith and Mercy stood on one side of their mother, Hope and Charity on the other. Lily and Emma leaned over the railing.

"Someone threw a rock through the kitchen window," Cook cried. "It nearly hit me in the head!"

Hope started down the stairs, but her father stopped her.

"Stay where you are," he ordered. "Don't *any-one* move!"

Suddenly there came a loud pounding on the front door.

"We hear that General Howe's sweetheart is giving a ball tonight, Master Hewson," a man shouted.

"We heard you were going. So we've fetched you a fine new coat to wear," someone else shouted.

Laughter echoed from all around the front of the house.

"Not a coat made of your expensive English cloth brought over on one of your ships, mind you, but one made right here in the colonies!" taunted another. "How do you fancy you'll look dancing the minuet in a coat made of tar and feathers?"

There was more laughter.

Master Hewson's face grew taut as the voices from the other side of the door became louder and more brazen.

"I hear it's all the fashion this year," another heckled.

More loud laughter and jeering was followed by more shattering of glass, then more rocks crashed through upstairs windows. Faith and Hope screamed. Little Charity hid behind her mother's skirts. Lily pulled Emma close.

"A Tory is someone with his head in England, his body in America, and his neck in need of a noose!" someone shouted gleefully.

"Why should they mean us such harm, William?"

Mistress Hewson cried. "We are loyal citizens. Why do they hate us so?"

"Calm yourself, my dear," Master Hewson called up to her. "We must stay calm." But everyone could hear the fear in his voice.

"Tell them we've done nothing but follow the law." Mistress Hewson's voice was rising to a shrill pitch. "Tell them our daughter is ill! Tell them to leave us alone! Tell them! Tell them!"

"They are no more than common rabble," Master Hewson said, trying to calm her. "They only mean to frighten us. It will do no good to answer such evil threats. The soldiers will surely pass by soon and come to our aid."

No one spoke as they hoped for the sound of a soldier's drum, but there was only the constant pounding on the door. It grew louder and louder, until Lily was certain the door itself would be torn from its hinges.

But just as suddenly as the pounding had started, it stopped. An eerie silence followed. No one in the house dared to speak or to move — until they heard a familiar little voice from the other side of the door.

"Lily! Emma! They won't let me back in. Please help me, Emma! Lily! Please!"

"That's Katie!" Lily and Emma cried out as they rushed to the door.

"We've got our tar pot full and a bag of feathers to go with it," a voice shouted from the other side. "I say, if the master won't wear the jacket, this little wench will."

"Help!" Katie yelled. "Help!"

"We've got to get her now!" said Lily.

"It's too dangerous for any of you out there," Master Hewson said. He put his hand on the doorknob.

"William, no!" Mistress Hewson screamed.

"Don't go, Papa!" cried Hope and Mercy.

But Master Hewson paid them no mind, and before they could stop him, he unlocked the bolt, stepped outside, and slammed the door shut behind him.

TWENTY-THREE

Into the Lion's Den

REDCOATS! MATT WAS SURE OF IT. HE HEARD
them before he saw them. The men's angry voices
filled the frigid night air. Had they come to arrest
him and Thomas — or to string them up right here?

Silently, Matt inched his way closer to the front
of the house, staying well hidden between the hedges.
He could see that they weren't soldiers at all, but
rather a group of men in ragged clothing, carrying
torches and waving clubs. They had formed a tight
circle around something, but Matt couldn't see what
or who was inside of it.

He heard one of the men shout, "You Tory
trash!" Another yelled, "Go back to your King!"

It was then that Matt realized they were
Patriots!

What were they doing at the Hewsons' house?
Were they there to hurt them? he wondered. There

was no time to find out. Thomas was depending on him to get to the party and complete their mission. General Washington was depending on him, too. Silently, Matt stole through the bushes, unnoticed by the angry mob. He made his way to the party.

The cobblestones, licked by an icy drizzle, shimmered in the lamplight. The houses he passed were dark, with most windows shuttered but for a few flickering candles burning behind the thick, wavy glass.

At the end of the block he saw one house that stood out from all the others, just as Thomas said it would. Every window blazed and dazzled with light. Carriages lined the street. The sound of music and gay laughter floated out from the open front door. Without a doubt, this was the house!

Matt slipped his hand into his pocket and felt for the wooden button and the gold coin. He made his way to the side door. He took a deep breath before lifting the brass knocker. Seconds later, a pudgy man with a large red nose and a white wig appeared.

Matt studied the man, who stared coldly back. "Wolf Hunter," Matt whispered, his insides running cold.

"Wolf Hunter? You?" the butler whispered, looking him up and down. "They're bigger fools than I thought. Have you the gold piece?"

Matt handed him the coin. The butler bit it, and when it proved to be real, he greedily shoved it into his pocket.

"The sleeves on this coat will be too big for you," he told Matt. "You'll have to turn up the cuffs. I'll give you some rags to stuff the shoes so you don't trip. And this wig will probably be too big as well, but you'll have to manage." He handed Matt his disguise.

Once Matt had changed, he glanced at his reflection in the window and was glad that his friends could not see him in a wig and ruffled clothes. Then he went to the kitchen, where the butler gave him a tray of glasses filled with red punch.

"The musicians are playing the third minuet already, and the dancers will want refreshments," the butler told Matt. "I have three others serving tonight, so just follow their lead. Move around the room. Hold the tray steady while the guests help themselves to a glass. Mind, you are a servant in this house. Look no one in the eye, and make no conversation. A good servant is invisible."

"What about the man with the scar?" Matt asked. "Where do I find —"

But the butler raised his hand to stop him. "I know nothing about the plans you and your lot have cooked up, and I will take no part in them. The gold piece is all I bargained for. What you do beyond serving the punch is your own business."

He led the way through a hallway and into a large room where they were met by a crowd of joyful revelers. Women in billowing skirts of colorful satins and silks sailed past, their smiling faces painted clown-white with circles of crimson on their cheeks. Old, snuff-nosed men with lace at their necks and gaudy ribbons at their knees traded talk about the price of cod and the latest cures for gout.

Heads were heaped with mounds of white curls, and the air was thick with the tang of spice. People milled around the dance floor as the keys of a harpsichord plinked out popular ballads.

But what caught Matt's eye was the sea of scarlet jackets. English officers stood in groups, stiff as last year's cornstalks in their bloodred coats and white trousers. He was in the heart of a Loyalist party! How on earth would he ever find the man he was looking for?

A woman led a tall officer wearing a haughty look on his face to Matt.

"Ah, General Howe, will you try our punch?" the woman asked.

Matt stared in disbelief. It was really General Howe! He nodded and reached for a glass from Matt's tray. Matt stared at the British commander who had kept Boston hostage and the rebels on the run. Not only was Matt in the lion's den, but here was the lion himself, a mere three inches away! If Matt was discovered here, he would surely be hung for treason!

There are to be no mistakes! Matt remembered Thomas telling him. *No mistakes at all!*

TWENTY-FOUR

Tar and Feathers

BACK AT THE HEWSONS' HOUSE, THE REBELS'
attack raged.

"Papa!" screamed Mercy from the upstairs
landing.

"Come back, Papa! Please come back!" Hope
and Faith cried. Charity sobbed beside them. Downstairs, Lily and Emma raced into the sitting room,
where Mistress Hewson and Cook were peering out
the windows.

The girls looked out to find a small group of
men in the street wielding torches, clubs, and iron
pokers. Their eyes were wild and angry. And like a
pack of mad dogs about to attack, they had formed
a circle around their prey.

Katie cowered in front of the men, frozen in
fear. She looked so tiny and helpless. A large, fierce-
looking man grabbed her by her wrists. The moment

Master Hewson stepped out of the door, the shouts of the angry mob rose.

"Seize him! Seize him!" someone cried.

"William Stafford, Daniel Healy. You are my neighbors. I beg of you, let the girl go," Master Hewson cried out to the men in the crowd.

"Begging, are you?" one of the men heckled. "How does it feel, now that the tables are turned? We've been begging your General Howe for months now to show us some mercy. But little good it did us. Our harbor is still closed, and our children are starving. And you dare ask for mercy?"

"The girl is not even my child!" Master Hewson told them.

"Matt! I want my brother!" Katie screamed.

"We didn't come for the child," a man said, stepping out of the crowd. "We've come for you, Hewson, and now we have what we want." He turned to the man holding Katie. "Unhand her."

The moment they let Katie go, she ran for the house. But her ankle was still weak and throbbing, and she tripped and fell. As she struggled back up, the twins hurried outside to rescue her. They carried Katie back into the house, and Mistress Hewson bolted the door once again.

"I was so scared," Katie sobbed. "Those bad men hurt my arm."

"They're animals," Mistress Hewson whispered, her lip quivering.

But they are Patriots! Lily thought. *They are supposed to be the good ones!*

Everyone rushed back to the sitting room window. From there they saw the kindhearted Master Hewson trying desperately to reason with the mob. He tried to talk above their shouts, but they only jeered louder. The circle grew tighter. Master Hewson shielded his face with his hands as one of the men knocked off his wig. Another bound him with rope.

Inside, Mistress Hewson covered her eyes with her hands. "Oh, dear Lord, help him! They mean to kill him!"

"Papa! Papa!" the children wailed from the stairs.

Lily's legs went weak as she watched the men rip off Master Hewson's shirt, take a pot of steaming tar, and pour it over Master Hewson's head and torso! As he writhed in pain, they emptied a sack of feathers over him. Then, with ropes, they hoisted him up on a cart and drove down the street, with the angry mob running behind them.

The family watched in horror as the cart disappeared down an icy lane.

"Papa," little Charity cried. "Bring back my papa!"

TWENTY-FIVE

The Bell, the Button, and the Spy

GENERAL HOWE PICKED UP A DRINK FROM Matt's tray. Matt tried to still his shaking hands as the glasses on his tray began to rattle and clatter. He quickly moved on before General Howe could notice. Matt hadn't gotten far when another pair of officers stopped him for some punch.

"I hear they hung a young man from Beer Lane for treason just yesterday," one remarked, taking a glass from Matt's tray and giving him a sideways look. "Arrested and executed without so much as a trial."

"A filthy spy, no doubt," the other noted. "They deserve no better."

Matt moved forward with his tray, studying each man he saw as he slowly circled the room. He could see it was going to be hard to spot the man in the red uniform with the scar and the missing button, since most of the men in the room wore the British uniforms of red wool. Time passed. More women in silks and satins glided by, as did more men in bright red uniforms.

Suddenly, and without warning, Matt hiccupped loudly! His face grew hot with embarrassment, then dread, as he remembered Thomas saying, *Whatever you do, don't draw attention to yourself.*

Matt squeezed his eyes shut and held his breath to ward off the next hiccup that he felt coming on. And that's when he collided with a woman who was strolling toward him! Four full glasses flew from his tray. Punch and shattered glass sprayed everywhere. The woman let out a shriek and slid on the slippery floor. She landed on her backside.

"My stars! I think I shall faint!" the woman cried out. "Catch that impudent rascal!"

The crowd went deadly silent. Even the musicians stopped playing. Every eye in the room had turned to Matt and the woman.

"My dear Mistress Streep, are you hurt?" an older officer exclaimed, rushing to the woman's rescue. He turned to Matt and picked him up by the collar. "What the deuce are you doing, boy?" he growled, giving Matt a rough shake.

Matt was too startled to answer. But the shock rid him of his hiccups. Seconds later, the butler shoved him into the kitchen. "Now get a fresh tray, you clumsy oaf!" the butler growled.

The music started again, and the crowd's chatter and laughter resumed with it. A footman handed Matt another tray filled with glasses.

"Here," he said. "Take these and have a care!"

Matt returned to the ballroom, anxious to find the man with the missing button. But as he looked across the room, his frustration grew. The room was awash with soldiers in red coats!

"I'll have a glass of that punch," a low, whispery voice interrupted his thoughts. Matt turned to find himself face-to-face with yet another man wearing the scarlet jacket of a British officer. But he noted a purposeful glint in the man's eyes, as well as the long scar that ran along the upper edge of his cheek.

"Clumsy of you, back there," the man said, never taking his eyes off of Matt. He reached for a glass of punch on Matt's tray. His hand lingered.

Matt silently scanned the four rows of gold brocade that ran around the soldier's sleeve. He counted three buttons and saw the short strand of red thread where the fourth button should have been. He raised his eyes and met the man's gaze full on.

That was him! Matt was sure of it. The scar, the missing button, and the look in the man's eye, all told him he was the one.

The guests were busy pairing off for the next waltz. Now was the time to act.

"I see you are missing a button, sir." The words tumbled out of his mouth. Matt fought to keep his hands steady as he waited for the man to make his move.

The man's steely blue eyes swept over the crowd. He picked up a drink and quickly drained his glass. "Yes, I am," the man answered. "And I would be glad for another."

Matt's throat went dry, and his heart raced. He could barely remember what to do next. He fumbled in his pocket for the button. Where was it? He switched the tray to his other hand and reached into his other pocket. There it was! He grasped it securely and placed the button on the tray.

"I say, this punch is quite good." The man's voice was calm and smooth as silk. He set his empty glass down, silently scooped up the button, and replaced it with another, all in one fluid movement. Then he stepped away from the tray.

Matt stared down at the shiny brass disc. All he had to do now was to pick up the button and put it into his pocket. He was slowly moving his hand up to the tray, when he felt a large hand on his shoulder!

"I'll have one of those," a new voice ordered.

Matt looked up. Another British officer reached for a glass on the tray. A panicky, gasping sound escaped Matt's throat as the soldier's white-gloved fingers grazed over the button!

"What's this? Are they serving buttons with their brew?" the officer asked.

Sweat gathered at the edges of Matt's wig. He looked around for the scar-faced man, hoping he would come to his rescue, but he had disappeared back into the crowd.

Meanwhile, the officer had removed his white gloves. One look at his hand and Matt's blood ran cold. For there on the back of his right palm was a small dark mole, a mole in the perfect shape of a bell!

Matt felt a sickly twist in his stomach as he recognized the surveyor from the coach, now dressed in a wig and a British officer's uniform. Thomas had been right after all. The man was no surveyor but a soldier working as a spy for the Crown. And before Matt could stop him, the British spy scooped up the button from the tray, tucked it into his pocket, and smiled a snakelike smile.

TWENTY-SIX

After Midnight

ALL WAS LOST IN THE BLINK OF AN EYE. IT happened so fast. It was exactly what Thomas had warned Matt not to do. He had let the button get into the wrong hands, into the hands of the Crown's spy!

"Did you see the rebel traitors on parade today?" Matt heard another officer ask the spy.

"Yes, and a grim parade it was," the spy replied.

"Grim it may be, but a necessary business," the soldier replied. "If you ask me, the Crown would do well to invest in more rope. String them all up, I say, and be done with them."

Frantic with worry, Matt lowered his head, fearful that the spy might recognize him from the coach. Meanwhile, he had to get the button back, but how would he do that? When the spy turned on his heel and walked away with the button in his pocket, Matt summoned all his courage and followed him.

"Excuse me, sir," he said.

The spy swung back around and stared at him hard. "Do I know you, boy?"

"I — I don't think so," Matt sputtered, his cheeks burning. "But I think you might have —"

"Have mistaken my button for one of your own, sir," the scar-faced man said, coming up behind them. A tense moment followed as the two men's eyes locked and they sized each other up. But the spy made no move to return the button.

"Of course, my stop at Lamb's Tavern before the ball and the four glasses of punch I've had here since have combined to render me unfit to be one hundred percent certain," the scar-faced man said, suddenly slurring his speech. He weaved back and forth, leaning on the other man's arm. "Sorry, old chap, I seem to be falling apart." He lifted his sleeve with the missing button and waved it in the air. "Buttons falling off like musket balls on a battle-field, aye? Perhaps you know of a good seamstress, sir. One who's willing to sew on a button or two? And if she be comely, well, all the better."

The other man's face relaxed. "You need to sober up, friend, or you'll be losing more than your but-tons." He reached into his pocket and produced the large brass button, then handed it over to the scar-faced man.

"Excellent advice, my dear fellow," the scar-faced man said, thrusting the button into his own pocket. "I shall retire to my rooms at once and put on a kettle of tea. Now, there's a drink to curl a grandmother's hair, aye?"

The two men laughed at the joke. But the British spy glanced back at Matt, and his gaze lingered, as if he was trying to recall the face before him. Matt bowed his head and pretended to check the glasses on his tray. It was then that he noticed the button. Somehow the scar-faced man had slipped it back onto his tray!

Matt grabbed the button and quickly pressed it safely into the bottom of his pocket. He had it! He had the information that he'd promised Thomas he would bring him! Now all he had to do was get out of the lion's den alive.

"Do you suppose we can convince the musicians to play one last minuet?" he overheard a woman ask.

"Well, my dear, we can try, though it is nearly midnight," replied her dancing partner.

Almost midnight? Was it possible? Had so much time gone by?

Matt heard Thomas's warning in his head. *Whatever you do, you must get back here by midnight!*

TWENTY-SEVEN

Huzzah!

THE MUSICIANS PLAYED THE LAST DANCE, AND as the candles burned down to stubs, their warm amber glow gave way to a chilly, dark room. Matt rushed into the pantry just off the kitchen. He set down his tray, kicked off his shoes, and hurried out of his footman's disguise. He quickly got back into his own clothes, then slipped out the side door, being careful not to be seen. Once outside, he broke into a run, keeping his hand in his pocket and his fingers tightly wrapped around the button.

He was nearly home when he heard a muffled moan coming from the side of the road. He stopped and peered down at something that caught his eye in the bright moonlight. What was it? Was it an animal? Was it a bird? Matt couldn't tell. But whatever it was, it was alive and covered in feathers!

"Help me! Please help me!" the voice cried out to him. The frightening-looking creature was a man!

Matt knelt down beside him. "I'll get someone to help you," Matt said. "Where do you live?"

The man clutched Matt's hand with the little strength he had left, and he held on tight.

"I live on Milk Street . . . and I need to get back to my family. . . . They are in terrible danger."

Matt took a closer look at the man covered in feathers. He had been beaten so badly it was hard to see who he was. Then Matt realized that the man was Master Hewson! But he didn't recognize Matt.

"You can lean on me," Matt told him. "Do you think you can stand?"

Master Hewson seemed to be fading out of consciousness.

Matt tried to prop him up, but his body had become a dead weight, and he wouldn't budge.

"Tell my wife . . . she and our children must get to safety," he whispered hoarsely. "Tell them . . . they must all be brave. . . ."

"You can tell them yourself when we get home," Matt said. "Just put your arms around my shoulders. We can make it home together."

But Master Hewson just closed his eyes. "Tell them that they are everything to me . . . and that I love them. . . ." His tar-blackened hand opened and the cracked pennywhistle he was gripping fell to the snowy ground.

"No, please," Matt whispered. "Please don't die." Tears froze on Matt's cheeks in the icy night air. "This wasn't supposed to happen. Thomas and Harry and the Patriots had wanted to change the world. But not like this! Not like this . . ."

"Halt! Who goes there?" a gruff voice called out in the dark.

Two soldiers in red coats walked toward them. One held a lantern, while the other pointed his musket at Matt.

Did someone see him exchange the button at the party? Had they sent a patrol to arrest him? Matt slid his hand into his pocket and once again gripped the button tightly in his hand. There was no time to run. He was trapped!

"Good God, man!" one of the soldiers exclaimed when he saw Master Hewson. "This must be the poor chap from Milk Street we heard about." The soldier looked at Matt. "Did you see it happen, boy?"

Matt shook his head. "I was working at the party down the street."

The soldier sighed. "Well, you better hurry home. These streets are not safe with the likes of such men who would do this to their own neighbor. We'll call for a wagon to pick up the body. His family will want him home."

"And a sad homecoming 'twill be," the other soldier said. "Go on now, lad, and be off with you."

Matt raced down the street. He had to get home before the soldiers found the coffin-maker's wagon in front of the Hewsons' house. He and Thomas had to leave before they were discovered. Matt ran faster than he'd ever known he could. He was running for his life.

Matt heard the coffin-maker's wagon before he saw it. The loud clatter of wheels and horses' hooves was followed by the light of lanterns swinging through the dark. The wagon, piled high with coffins, came to a stop before the Hewsons' front door. The driver eyed Matt suspiciously.

"I thought there would be two of you," the driver rasped.

"There are two of us," Matt told him. "Can you just wait while I go up and get the other one?"

"I'll not risk waiting more than a few minutes," the driver warned.

Matt raced toward the back door. He heard voices coming from the front rooms, but the kitchen was dark and empty. He took Katie's little pink flashlight out of his pocket and used it to find his way up the darkened stairway.

He slipped back into the attic bedroom and

was surprised to find Mistress Hewson sitting on the bed beside Thomas. Her face was streaked with tears.

"Where were you, boy?" she asked.

"I — I —" Matt stammered. He looked at Thomas, but his eyes were closed, and he didn't stir. "I ran an errand for Thomas," Matt finally said. "It was something he needed."

"What he needs now is rest and our prayers," Mistress Hewson said gravely.

"But we have to go," Matt told her. "The man with the wagon is waiting outside for us." Matt took a step toward the bed. "Thomas, you have to wake up!" he shouted. "You have to wake up now!"

Thomas moaned weakly but he didn't open his eyes.

Mistress Hewson grabbed Matt by the shoulder and pulled him away from the bed. "For God's sake, boy, leave him be," she cried. "They've taken my husband — God knows what they've done to him — and they killed my brother Harry. I'll not lose another to this war. You must go without him. I will see that no harm comes to him."

Matt's heart sank as he stole a look back at the young spy, willing him to open his eyes.

"Do you know my brother well?" Mistress Hewson asked.

"He's my friend," Matt whispered hoarsely. "We had a plan. We were going to set the world right together."

"Oh, how I wish you had," Mistress Hewson murmured. "How I wish you had."

Matt tried to muster the courage to tell Mistress Hewson about her husband, and to give her his message.

"You and your children must leave here at once," Matt began. "For on my way here . . ."

But Mistress Hewson put her finger on Matt's lips to silence him.

"Shh . . . not now, lad," she said. "My brother needs quiet. Let's let him rest."

A horse whinnied impatiently outside the window, and Matt realized there was no time to waste. If he was going to get back to the mill, he would have to leave right now.

Matt looked back at Thomas. His eyes opened slowly, and he motioned for Matt to come closer.

"Give us a moment, will you, Martha?" Thomas whispered. His sister stepped out of the room, and Matt approached the bed.

"Tell me . . ." Thomas said weakly. "Were you . . . successful?"

Matt nodded. "I have the button right here in my pocket."

Thomas let out a sigh of relief. "Good, lad . . . I knew you could do it."

"The wagon is waiting outside for us," Matt urged. "We have to leave right now."

But Thomas shook his head. "Give the button to my men at the mill. They will know what to do with it."

"But what about you?" protested Matt. "The redcoats are coming. What if they find you here?"

"Don't worry about me. You've still got the mission to complete. You must get out safely. Go now and take care. And guard that button with your life."

"I will," Matt promised. "But please, can't you come with me?"

Thomas reached for Matt's hand and gave it a squeeze. "I'm proud of you, Matthew." His breath was labored. "Matthew . . . that's a good strong name you've got there, lad. . . ." His voice trailed off. "A good . . . strong . . . name . . ."

Mistress Hewson came back into the room and put her hand on Matt's shoulder. "Leave him, son. He needs to rest now."

Matt bolted out the door without looking back. He raced down the stairs and out to the street. The driver was standing next to his wagon.

"Well, where is he, then?" the driver demanded. "I can't wait any longer."

"You don't need to," Matt said sadly. "It's just going to be me."

The driver climbed up into the wagon. He opened one of the long wooden boxes and waited for Matt to get in. Matt hesitated, but only for a second, for he could hear a distant clatter of wheels on cobblestones. Another wagon was coming down the street.

Matt hurried into the coffin. The lid was closed, and with it came total darkness. The strong smell of fresh-cut pine filled his nose. Matt opened his eyes wide, hoping for any bit of light, straining to hear every sound. But sadness and panic seemed to be the only things to seep in. What if he had an itch? What if he wanted to move? What if he needed more air?

He tried to calm himself with thoughts of Hooter, Tony, and Q, and how happy they'd be to see him. But what would become of Thomas? Would he live? Would the redcoats find him?

The rest of the trip was a blur of being knocked up and down and fighting to hold his sadness and panic at bay — until the wagon finally bumped to a stop.

When the driver lifted the coffin's lid, Matt took a long, deep breath of the cold fresh air. He couldn't stand up fast enough. Once on the ground, he saw the familiar stone building with the large wooden waterwheel at its side. Smoke poured out of the chimney, and the dust-caked windows glowed from the firelight within. He was back at Sutton's Mill! Matt noticed a big, beautiful white horse tied up at a hitching post with eight other horses beside it. Whose were they? he wondered.

The mill door opened, and a rebel came out with Tony, Hooter, and Q following behind him. Hooter let out a loud whoop on seeing Matt. Tony couldn't stop talking. Q couldn't stop grinning.

"But where is Thomas?" the rebel asked.

"He's at his sister's house on Milk Street," Matt said, biting his lip. "He was hurt so badly, he couldn't make the trip."

The man sighed loudly. "How?" he whispered. "The redcoats?"

"Yes," Matt told him. "And they killed his brother, too."

The man winced, as if he'd been slapped across the face. "And the information Harry was to exchange?"

"I made the exchange for him," Matt said.

The man's eyebrows shot up. "You?" the man asked. He stared at Matt long and hard. "You'd better come with me right away!"

Matt and the boys followed the man down the stairs to the mill's lower floor, which had recently been filled with cannons and guns. But the room was now empty, except for a table and some chairs. Two lamps burned brightly on the table. The smell of wood smoke rose from the bright flames in the grate.

A tall, stately man was sitting before the hearth. In the firelight Matt recognized the statuesque figure in the blue wool coat and buff trousers at once. He wore no wig, but his sandy brown hair was tied in a ponytail at the nape of his neck. His regal air and steady gaze were unmistakable. Matt knew that they were looking, once again, at General George Washington!

The rebel approached the General and whispered something into his ear. The famous man shook his head, his face reddening. "How many more fine young men will they cut down?" he shouted. He pounded the table with his fist.

The room went deadly silent. The General stared into the fire. When he looked back up, his eyes fell on the boys. "So which of you was the brave lad who attended a rather special party tonight?" he asked.

"I guess that would be me, sir," Matt said.

The famous man nodded. "And I hear you came away with a small" — he cleared his throat and smiled slyly — "memento?"

Matt continued to stare, too nervous to answer. Then he remembered the button.

He took it out of his pocket, and with shaking hands, he passed it along to the famous leader.

A small well-dressed black man named William who stood at the General's side offered his knife, and General Washington used it to pry off the button's false bottom. He carefully worked the knife around the tiny, tightly rolled paper and lifted it out. Matt watched as he moved to the table and held the paper over the lit candle. Matt held his breath. A tense silence followed. Everyone's eyes were on the General and the paper in his hands.

What did the words say? Matt wondered. Was it good news or bad? The General's face showed no emotion. Finally, after several long minutes, he looked up and said, in a slow, deliberate voice, "They may have been dancing in Boston tonight, lads, but once they see the surprise we have in store for them, they won't be dancing for long. Thomas Jamison and his brother will not have fought in vain." The room erupted into cheers and loud huzzahs from the men.

"Well done, lad!" The General smiled.

"Yes, sir," Matt said. "Thank you, sir."

"Huzzah! Huzzah!" the men in the room all cried.

"Huzzah! Huzzah!" Hooter, Tony, and Q shouted, giving each other high fives.

Matt beamed with pride. The General shook his hand. "God willing, we will free Boston from the Crown's grip, and our colonies will only grow stronger. You've done a good night's work, boy. Get some rest now, for tomorrow will surely test all our mettle."

"Tomorrow?" Matt mumbled.

"And you, young man," the General said, turning to Hooter. "Are you a Patriot as well?"

"Oh, totally," Hooter said, throwing back his shoulders and standing as straight as he could.

The General silently looked him over and eyed his shoes. "Nice buckles," he said.

TWENTY-EIGHT

The Secret March

"WHERE ARE WE GOING?" MATT ASKED THE next morning as he and the boys were hustled into a cart with the men from the mill.

"Just do as you're told. The first stop is in the woods," one of the rebels said.

The boys spent the entire day helping the men gather tree limbs and logs in the forest and load them onto carts and wagons. They stopped only to take a drink of strong cider or a bite of oatcake. They were exhausted and starving.

By sundown, the four friends were on the road with large bundles of branches strapped to their backs. They followed behind a long line of wagons and horses, silently moving over the frozen ruts. It was slow going. The wagons' wheels were wrapped with straw to deaden their sound. And they were so top-heavy with wood, stone, and cannons that they threatened to topple over at every turn. General

Washington had ordered that no lamps were to be used and no fires lit. No one was to speak above a whisper.

The farther they walked, the more wagons they met. Hundreds of men and boys seemed to appear under the bright moonlight, their heads bent low, their backs laden with bundles of straw and wood.

After several hours trudging up a rocky hillside in the bitter cold, everyone came to a stop. As Matt and the boys waited for orders, they blew into their hands, which were raw and red from the cold.

"Where are we?" Hooter whispered.

"We're at the top of Dorchester Heights," a young stranger said, slipping a bundle of birch saplings off his back.

At the mention of Dorchester, Matt felt a wave of goose bumps spread over his skin, and he and the boys exchanged uneasy glances. The roar of cannon fire suddenly sounded from the distance.

"What's that?" Tony cried.

"I'll wager it's the cannon fire of Boston's own Henry Knox," a man beside them said with a smile. "He and our comrades in Roxbury are sending their greetings to the redcoats in Boston."

"Couldn't they just send a postcard?" Hooter whispered.

"It sounds awfully close," Matt whispered back as the bombardment continued.

"Don't worry, 'tis a good diversion," the man assured them.

But Matt was worried. What if the fighting got closer? What if a cannonball came crashing straight at them? Worse still, where were the girls? What if they were hit by rebel cannon fire?

"The redcoats will start firing back on our men soon," another man said. "Say a prayer they miss their marks. And say another that Howe doesn't send his thousands of troops up here after us."

"What would happen then?" Tony asked.

"It would be a slaughter," the man said grimly. "A bloody slaughter."

Matt felt his knees go weak. He nodded to his friends, and the four huddled close. "If only we knew what was going to happen next," Matt whispered to Q. "If only we knew if we won or lost at Dorchester."

"Don't look at me," Q said, shaking his head sadly. "You guys are the ones who wanted to throw marshmallows at army men rather than read a book — remember? I have no idea what will happen next."

"If only we had the book with us now," said Matt.

"If only we had the marshmallows with us now," Hooter sighed.

They trudged on, scared and exhausted, until suddenly the order came down, passed in a whisper from one man to the other. "Begin emptying the wagons. Make haste, but make no noise. And any man who makes a fire will be shot."

Matt and the boys followed the men's lead and began silently carting wood, straw, stones, and sand-filled barrels from the wagons to the hillside's frozen ledges. Others worked together to build up breastworks and to position barrels, rocks, and cannons.

The last wagon was not emptied until dawn. Matt stood with the others, exhausted and yet exuberant as they marveled at the work they had done. For the entire hillside was now ringed with mounds of rock and birch timber, each topped with one of Henry Knox's cannons, all pointing down at the King's transports in the harbor! Rows of barrels were ready to roll down upon any who dared to attack. It looked like the work of tens of thousands!

"What do you suppose General Howe will do when he wakes up and sees this?" Q whispered to a soldier.

"He'll either attack within the hour, or he'll wait for the cover of night," the soldier answered.

Which was it? the four boys wondered miserably. If only they'd read Q's book!

Matt and the boys hunkered down under the cover of a wagon's tarp. There they waited with the others all day. Everyone's ears pricked up as they listened for the sound of a bugle, the beat of a drum, or the sudden roar of cannon fire. But the only guns they heard were in the distance. That night, a fierce winter storm blew across Boston and blanketed the Heights with snow and freezing rain. Wintry blasts off the Atlantic continued to howl all through the next day.

Tony couldn't stop his teeth from chattering. Q complained that his fingers were growing numb. Matt moaned that he couldn't feel his toes. Hooter was so hungry that even the idea of eating a moldy oatcake sounded good to him.

They were all beginning to think they'd freeze to death when suddenly they heard someone shout.

"Howe will not attack! He has given orders to evacuate! The redcoats are leaving! The redcoats are leaving!"

Hooter threw off the tarp, and together the boys leaped to their feet to join in the boisterous chorus of cheers that broke out at the news. General Washington's plan had worked! The rebels had built such strong fortifications in one night that General

Howe's guns couldn't reach over the breastworks! Meanwhile, the English ships in the harbor were in the direct line of fire. Howe and his men were backing down and would soon be on the run.

A familiar tall figure in blue and buff suddenly appeared on a magnificent white steed. Everyone's eyes were on him as he slowly crossed the hillside. Then the General took off his hat and waved it to the men and boys who had worked so valiantly for him. "Well done, men! Well done!" General Washington cried.

A deafening cheer rose up and echoed over the hills. "Huzzah! Huzzah! Huzzah! Three cheers for General Washington! Three cheers for our good General!"

Everyone laughed and cried with joy. Hooter lifted Tony up off his feet and twirled him in the air.

"So now we know what happened at Dorchester," Q said with a grin.

"Yeah, we sure do," Matt agreed. "Now all we have to do is find Katie and the twins."

"And a way home," Tony added.

Home. The word lingered in the air. *Home.*

TWENTY-NINE

All Aboard!

THE HILLS OF DORCHESTER HUMMED WITH the many voices of the joyous men and boys who had worked so hard to defend them. Matt, Tony, Hooter, and Q hopped a ride on a wagon with two of Thomas's men. By sundown they were back at Sutton's Mill. But tired as they were, they couldn't stop talking about General Washington's army and their amazing feat. They'd beaten the British without a bloody battle!

The boys were now free to leave the mill, but the rebels warned that the city was still filled with redcoats and that it was too dangerous for travel.

"You are better off waiting here a few days until Howe and his troops have left Boston for good," one of them said with a weary smile. "We'll be back then to let you know when all is clear."

The men gave them some hardtack, oatcakes, and a jug of cider. They also shot two rabbits before they left and cooked them over the fire.

Hooter couldn't bear the thought of "eating the Easter bunny." But the others, in their starvation, succumbed to the rich, tasty aroma of the cooked meat. Once the men had gone, the boys set about surviving on their own. Matt and Hooter gathered wood, while Tony collected snow to melt for water. Q hunted for birch bark to make tea. "It's full of vitamin C," he announced.

"So now you're an expert on birch bark tea?" Tony asked.

"If you'd been paying attention, it was part of my oral report last month on American Indians surviving on the land," Q said smugly.

"Too bad you didn't do a report on making a pizza on the land," Hooter quipped.

Together, the boys were able to keep the fire going and stay warm. But each day that passed, Matt grew more and more worried. What if the rebels didn't come back for them? What would they do when the wood and the food ran out?

By the end of the week, despair had set in. When they had finally given up hoping for even the smallest ray of light, the mill door swung open. A Patriot in an oilskin coat and hat hurried inside from the pouring rain.

"Well, lads!" he exclaimed, shaking the water from his hat. "You can go now! The patrols have quit their posts, and Howe is gathering his troops to leave the city."

"But what happened to the Loyalists?" Matt asked, thinking of the Hewsons.

"They are running with their tails between their legs. And they can't run fast enough." The man grinned. "The roads are already crowded with their wagons and carts heading for the harbor. Howe has promised not to burn the city down if we hold back and let them leave in peace. You never saw so many white-faced, white-wigged cowards in all your life! Good riddance, aye?"

Where was Thomas? And where was his sister and her family? Matt wondered. How would they survive in a city that was about to be overtaken by their enemies?

"The patrols have quit their posts, and the roads are open," the man continued. "I've a horse and wagon waiting outside and will be going into the city if you are looking for a ride."

"Thanks," Matt tried to explain. "We came here by boat, but we lost it."

But the man shook his head. "It's most likely

stolen. People are lining up to pay a king's ransom for a seat on any vessel now. If I were you, I'd forget about your boat and look for a good larder to raid instead. There will be plenty of empty houses and food left for the taking, once the Tories flee."

The boys piled into the wagon, which bumped and rattled over the deep-rutted road into Boston. Matt's eyes darted from one building to the next and to all the dark spaces in between, anxious to catch any sight of the long-lost girls.

The horses slowed as they neared the center of the city. There the road was choked with carriages, carts, and wagons. Families on foot, their backs laden with bundles and baskets, hurried past. Everyone carried something. A small girl held a silver candlestick that was almost as big as she was. An old man clutched a birdcage in one hand and a footstool in the other. A young boy carried two gilded picture frames over each arm.

Women wept and wailed as featherbeds, blankets, and rugs were thrown out of open windows into wagons waiting below. Babies howled. Dogs barked. Men shouted. And the insistent "Hurry! Hurry! Hurry!" was on everyone's lips.

But no matter where he looked, Matt could find no trace of the girls.

News that George Washington had taken the Heights and General Howe's troops were packing to leave had spread quickly. The Patriots would soon be back in the city. Loyalists were running for their lives.

"Who-o-oah!" the driver called to the horses that bucked and whinnied. The wagon slowed to a stop. "You'd better get out here," he told the boys.

Matt, Hooter, Tony, and Q jumped down, and the driver snapped his whip. The wagon rolled slowly away. Matt's throat tightened at the sight of the panicked faces on the people pushing past.

Q nervously adjusted his glasses, while Tony hung on to Hooter for dear life.

"Clear the way! Clear the way! His Majesty's men coming through!" someone shouted.

Matt spun around to see a group of red-coated soldiers pulling a large cannon. The crowd parted to let them pass.

"That's what we need, more big guns. Let them have it!" shouted a man carrying a small boy in his arms.

"Has General Howe changed his mind?" another man hollered. "Are you getting into position to fire on those filthy rebels after all?"

But a burly British soldier squashed any such

hopes. "No, sir. We're headed for the harbor, with orders to sink all of our heavy guns into the sea."

A ripple of angry words and curses swept through the desperate crowd.

"We've got to get out of here!" Matt told the others as they clung to one another. But the narrow street was so packed with families, it was impossible to make any headway against the strong current of bodies pushing them forward.

They rounded a bend, where they saw white sails set against a blue sky. Long wooden sheds and rope walks flanked the sea-swept piers. Gulls cried overhead, and the breeze carried the sharp smell of tar and fish. They had reached the harbor.

Massive sailing ships with hundred-foot-tall masts were jammed between wooden boats of every size and shape. The vessels creaked and groaned loudly, swaying in their chains. As the boys were shoved forward, they looked desperately through the water at all the boats.

Meanwhile, the defeated Tory families pushed and pleaded to get onto the gangplanks. The air was thick with their panicked cries. But the soldiers kept them back with the constant command: "All passengers must wait for their turn to board! Stay calm and wait for your turn!"

The boys tried desperately to break free but were swept up in the crushing crowd. Before they knew it, they were trapped on a gangplank!

"After you four boys, no more can come!" a soldier commanded as he cut off a line behind them.

"Oh, no!" cried Matt. "There's no way off!"

"All aboard!" shouted a sailor. "All aboard!"

THIRTY

Pox on the Boat!

"EXCUSE ME, MA'AM," Q ASKED AN ELDERLY woman who was squeezed beside them on the ship's main deck. "Can you tell us where this ship is going?"

"'Tis bound for Halifax, lad," the woman answered. "And only Providence knows what we shall encounter on those godforsaken shores."

"Where's Halifax?" Tony whispered.

"Maybe it's warmer there," Hooter said with a shiver.

"Exceedingly unlikely," Q said, "since Halifax is in Canada and north of here."

"Only it's the Canada of 1776," Matt said, his stomach tightening into knots. The crowd shifted as people pressed in closer.

There was no escaping the desperate crowd's tight hold. The boys locked arms to keep from getting separated as the crush of people pulled them forward.

"We've got to get off this ship now!" Matt said, but he was distracted by a commotion that broke out just ahead of them.

"What is it?" one of the ship's crew called out.

"A child says she wants to get off," a woman answered.

"She's lucky to be on this boat, with or without a brother," someone else said.

Matt's ears pricked up at the word *brother*. He scanned the deck to see where the voices were coming from, but the tightly packed crowd blocked his view. That's when he heard a defiant little voice declare, "I want Matt!"

"Katie!" Matt shouted, pushing through the mass of bodies. And there, just a few feet ahead of him, was Katie! Emma and Lily were beside her, trying to convince her to stay on the boat.

"Katie!" Matt cried. He ran to her and picked her up in his arms. "Oh, Katie! I found you! I found you!"

"Matt! Matt!" Katie cried, clinging to her brother for dear life. "I didn't want to go without you. And now you are here!"

"Matt! Hooter!" Lily shrieked.

"Tony! Q!" screamed Emma. "Where were you? I can't believe we found you at last!" The children jumped up and down, laughing, hooting, and crying, as they hugged one another.

"We were afraid we'd never see you again!" Lily sobbed.

The children all talked at once, when Mercy, Hope, Faith, and Charity pushed their way toward them. The Hewson sisters' pretty faces were now washed in worry, and their rumpled clothes were mismatched layers of dresses and petticoats. Their merry chatter was replaced with sober silence as they clutched their hastily packed bundles.

"These boys are our friends," Lily explained to the Hewson girls. "Matt is Katie's brother, and they came with us on the boat — and then we all got separated."

"But what are *you* doing on this ship?" Matt asked.

"We came with the Hewsons," Emma said, nodding toward the Hewson girls. "We were staying with their family, and when the soldiers came and told everyone to leave the city, we had nowhere else to go."

"*Hewson*?" Matt asked. "The Hewsons from Milk Street — where Thomas Jamison lived?"

"How do you know my uncle?" Mercy asked.

"It's a long story," Matt sighed. He looked sadly at the Hewson girls. "I'm sorry for everything that happened to your family. But you should know that both your uncles just wanted to make a better country. The rebels are going to change things for the good — even though it doesn't seem that way now."

Mercy's dark eyes flashed. "Our father is dead, murdered by the mob. And our mother stayed behind to care for my sister and uncle. We may never see them alive again. Is that the change your Patriots wished for?"

Matt took a step back, startled by her words. "No," he said. "I know your uncles never wanted to hurt your family. They were good men."

"My father was a good man, too," Mercy lashed back.

"I was with your father when he died," Matt said. "He told me to tell you that he wants you to be brave — and to know how much he loves you."

There was an awkward silence, which Charity was the first to break. "I want Mama and Papa," she cried. "I don't want to be here with all of these strangers."

"Papa wants us to be brave, and so we must be," Mercy told her. "Besides, they're not all strangers. Katie, Lily, and Emma are coming with us."

"No," Matt corrected her. "Katie and the twins must get off of this ship now and come with *us*."

"Matt's right," Emma agreed. "We have to go with them. I'm sorry."

The Hewson girls looked stricken.

"We'll never forget all your family has done for us," Lily said gently, reaching out her pinky as she and Mercy touched thumbs in their secret handshake.

"Be safe, dear friend," Mercy whispered. "And I pray one day soon you'll all find your way back home."

"You, too," whispered Lily. "You, too."

And as the seven girls hugged tightly one last time, a bell rang out and a sailor cried, "Last call to leave the port!"

A hush fell over the noisy crowd as the passengers turned and silently gazed back toward the dock.

"What are they looking at?" Matt asked.

"Home," the man beside them said with a sad shake of his head. "We are taking a last look at the only place we have ever called home. For no Loyalist will be allowed back in the colonies once the rebels take root."

"Good-bye, Boston! Good-bye, Mama! Good-bye, dear Papa," the Hewson girls said through their tears.

"Good-bye, America!" the people called, their voices cracking with emotion.

"How are we going to get off this ship?" asked Q desperately as the bell signaled their departure.

"We'll never make it back to the gangplank," Tony said. "There are too many people in the way."

Emma looked down at her fingernails and got an idea. She took the bottle of nail polish out of her purse. Without wasting any time, she painted red spots on Katie's face. Then she held Katie in her arms.

"Clear the gangplanks!" a sailor shouted.

Lily went into action. "Help, us please!" she shrieked. "Our sister is sick with the pox!"

"Pox! Pox! Pox! That girl has the pox!" the whispers swept through the crowd. Seized with panic, people fell over one another in their hurry to get away from them. Then, like a miracle, the crowd parted, clearing the way on the gangplank! And in a moment, the seven children filed quickly and easily off of the boat.

Once on dry ground, they pushed through the swarms of people and soldiers still hoping to board. But as soon as anyone saw Katie's spotted face, they hurried out of her way. And they continued forward, until they finally left the crowds behind and reached an empty stretch of dock.

"Now what do we do?" asked Q. "We're free — but we have nowhere to go."

"Maybe we should walk along the water," suggested Hooter.

No one was paying attention to Katie as they discussed their next move. Katie amused herself by throwing stones into the harbor. She was pretending it was a wishing well, and she wished for their boat each time a stone splashed into the water. It was then that she saw a misty blue cloud rising from off of the water.

"Matt!" she shouted. "Look!"

"Not now, Katie. We're busy," Matt shushed her without even turning around.

"But the boat," Katie insisted. "We have to get into it."

"We just got off the boat," said Emma.

"Not the big boat," Katie said. "Our little boat." And everyone turned to find the old blue rowboat rocking ever so gently before them!

Silence fell over the seven children, their eyes glazed and trancelike, their expressions frozen, as they filed into the wooden craft. The blue mist rose up around them, and the boat shuddered and shook. No one moved a muscle as the old boat spun around and around and around — until it spun beyond time and space.

Then all was black.

THIRTY-ONE

Somewhere Over the Rainbow

MATT HELD TIGHTLY TO THE SIDES OF THE boat as he became aware of the world spinning and spinning around him. What was happening? Where were they going? He saw a blinding flash of light, and a shower of bright stars swirled around them in space. Then a wave of cold water crashed over them as the boat landed with a violent thud.

Katie was the first to open her eyes. She was clinging to Matt, terrified of being separated again. "Matt! I'm so dizzy," she cried. "Where are we?"

"My stomach hurts," Emma moaned.

"So does mine," Tony groaned. "I think I'm going to —" Before he could finish his sentence, he leaned over the side of the boat and threw up.

Matt pressed his hands to his forehead and tried to stop the spinning in his head. He thought he might throw up, too.

Katie looked around, trying to focus her eyes. Then she squinted up at the sky.

"Matt," she said. "What kinds of airplanes did they have back in colonial times?"

"Airplanes?" everyone said together. They all looked up into the blue sky and fell over one another, laughing and cheering and crying all at once. For there, flying just below the clouds and glinting merrily in the sun, was an airplane — an honest to goodness airplane!

"*Wa-hooo!*" Matt shouted.

"We did it!" Tony hollered. "We're home!"

"Look, it's our lake!" Lily cried, pointing across the familiar wide expanse of water.

"We're really here! We're really home!" exclaimed Katie.

Then they all laughed at the spots on Katie's face.

"It feels so good to be back!" Emma said.

"Exceedingly good," murmured Q.

Hooter sniffed the air. "I can almost smell the hot dogs."

"Actually, what you smell is diesel fuel from the motorboats," Q corrected him.

"It smells delicious to me." Hooter closed his eyes and smiled. "I'll eat anything that's not a moldy oatcake."

"Welcome back to the twenty-first century, everyone," Q said.

Then Hooter looked down at his feet. "My shoes," Hooter cried. "I've lost Ben's shoes!"

"Ben who?" Katie asked. "What are you talking about?"

"Ben Franklin, that's who," Hooter groaned. "I had a pair of shoes that belonged to Ben Franklin!"

"Are you serious?" Lily asked.

"Totally serious," Hooter moaned. "And he has my sneakers. We traded."

"The centrifugal force from the spinning boat must have knocked them off your feet," said Q.

Hooter picked up the oars and began to row. The boat gently glided over the calm lake, and everyone grew quiet at the sight of the familiar jumble of aluminum-sided houses that clung to the shore. They silently passed by the many black-topped driveways, minivans, motorcycles, and cars. Every yard seemed to be crammed with plastic picnic furniture, barbecue grills, swing sets, bright-colored toys, tubes, and rafts. It was all so different from the other America, the one they had just returned from.

"I wonder what happened to the Hewsons," Lily said with a catch in her throat.

"We can Google them when we get home," suggested Q.

"They were so nice. It still seems strange to think that they were America's enemies," Emma said.

"How do such good people get to be your enemies?" Lily wondered aloud.

"I don't know," Matt said quietly. "I guess war is like that. People just choose sides."

"They sure chose the wrong side," added Tony.

"But it didn't seem wrong to them," Lily insisted. "The Hewsons were born in America. They just chose to stay loyal to their king. Isn't loyalty supposed to be a good thing?"

"But if everyone had stayed loyal to King George, we wouldn't have the democracy we have today," Q pointed out.

"It took brave men, like Thomas and his brother, to create our country," Matt said.

"And don't forget Ben Franklin," Hooter added.

"But Master Hewson was brave, too," Emma said. Everyone was quiet then.

"I thought choosing sides would be so simple, but it's not," Lily finally said, and Matt agreed.

"Well, I'm not going to have any problem choosing what to do when I get home," Hooter said. "First I'll choose to open the fridge and make a sandwich.

I'll probably choose the bologna over the turkey and the potato chips over the carrot sticks my mom is always trying to get me to eat."

Everyone laughed, for those were choices they were all eager to make.

As Hooter rowed them across the lake, they grew thoughtful again.

"It's hard to believe that this old rowboat really took us back in time," Lily said.

"It is woefully untechnological-looking for a time-travel vehicle," Q agreed.

"But it works," Matt said. "I'll never forget meeting Thomas and General Washington."

"I'll never forget the march to Dorchester," Tony added.

"And I'll never forget meeting Ben Franklin — and wearing his shoes," Hooter sighed.

"He looked so funny in your sneakers," Q said.

Hooter smiled at the memory. "He really liked them, didn't he? He said they made his bunions feel better. What's a bunion, anyway?"

"A bunion is a growth on the foot. . . ." Q began a lengthy definition of a bunion when he was interrupted by the familiar tinny melody of "Somewhere Over the Rainbow," coming from Emma's purse.

Everyone stopped and stared at the phone that was now in Emma's hand.

"It's my mom!" she cried excitedly, looking down at the screen. She couldn't wait to hear the sound of her mother's voice. She put her phone on SPEAKER so Lily could hear her, too. But what they heard was not the welcoming greeting they were expecting.

"EMMA ROSE CAPELL! WHERE IN HEAVEN'S NAME HAVE YOU BEEN!" Mrs. Capell demanded. "YOUR DINNER WAS READY AN HOUR AGO! YOU GIRLS BETTER COME HOME THIS INSTANT BEFORE I GROUND YOU FOR A WEEK! I'VE BEEN CALLING EVERYONE IN THE NEIGHBORHOOD LOOKING FOR YOU!"

"Oh, Mom!" Emma said, as she lovingly pressed the phone next to her cheek. "We're really sorry. We'll make it up to you. We'll be home in a few minutes. We were fooling around, and Katie hurt her ankle, and we sort of got . . . carried away."

"I'll say we got carried away," Tony whispered. "Far away!"

"Is Katie all right?" Mrs. Capell's voice was full of concern.

"She's fine," Emma assured her. "She's right here with us and the boys."

"Well, I'm calling you from town. We ran out of milk, and I still have to drop off the dry cleaning," Mrs. Capell continued. "You can let yourselves in and reheat your dinner in the microwave. Everything is in the fridge — so don't fill up on junk food."

"Oh, junk food, how I've missed you!" Hooter sighed, rubbing his palms together and licking his lips.

"And the next time you feel like getting carried away, you're going to be in BIG trouble," Mrs. Capell went on.

"I'm so sorry, Mom," Emma said again, then hung up the phone.

Hooter steered the boat back to the cove, where they pulled up behind the brush. But the moment they all piled out, they heard a loud hissing sound. And with a flash of bright light, the rowboat once again disappeared.

"I wonder where it's going now," whispered Matt.

"Probably to another place that doesn't have cars, or computers, or bathrooms," predicted Q.

"Speaking of bathrooms," Tony said.

"Bathrooms!" they all shouted together, and they raced, fast as lightning, to the Capells' sprawling modern house by the water. Then they burst through the back door and charged around the house together, flipping on lights, flushing toilets, and turning on faucets. They pressed the buttons on electric toothbrushes and switched on blow-dryers. They laughed and cheered on hearing the familiar hums and purrs of the modern gadgets they had missed so much.

"It's like we've died and gone to heaven," Hooter said, opening a kitchen cabinet and staring at the shelves filled with fresh food. He helped himself to a jar of Marshmallow Fluff and a bag of potato chips. He dipped the chips into the marshmallow and stuffed as many as he could into his mouth at a time. The other children gobbled up fresh fruit that sat in a bowl on the counter, alternating with crackers, cheeses, guacamole, and a big carton of ice cream.

Lily took a pizza from the freezer and put it into the microwave. She also reheated the dinners her mother had left in the refrigerator.

No one was talking. They were too busy eating.

Emma handed out juice boxes to everyone, and they raised them in a toast.

"Huzzah! Huzzah!" they all cheered.

When Q spotted the laptop on the counter, he left the table and turned it on. The others followed and gathered around him, looking eagerly over his shoulder. Q sighed happily as his fingers flew over the keys. "Ah, to bask once again in the warm glow of a computer screen," he murmured. Everyone held their breath as Q typed: "The Battle of Dorchester."

"It says here that taking back Boston was an important win for General Washington in the Revolution," Q said excitedly.

"And we were there to help!" Hooter said proudly, remembering the glorious view of Boston they had from the hills.

"Try *Thomas Jamison*," Matt requested.

Once again, Q's fingers flew over the keys. "There's a Thomas Jamison, born in Boston in 1751, who died in 1811, coming up on a genealogy site. Looks like the Jamison family tree."

"Thomas was twenty-five years old," Matt said.

Q did a quick calculation in his head. "Which means he was born in 1751. That's got to be your Thomas," he grinned.

"Then he didn't die from his wounds," Matt said. "And he lived a long time after that."

"He had a big family, too," Lily added, leaning over Tony to look at the screen. "Look — he and his wife, Sarah, had five daughters and a son named Harry Matthew Jamison."

"Harry Matthew?" Matt whispered.

"Do you think he was named after you?" Emma asked.

Matt beamed. "I don't know. But Matthew is a good strong name."

"Try Charity Hewson," said Katie, as Q flipped back to the Dorchester site. But before he could reply, the doorbell rang. Lily ran to answer it. It was Tony's father.

"Your mother said you fellows were over here," Mr. Manetti said, walking into the kitchen. "What's going on? And what on earth happened to your face, Katie?"

Katie touched the red spots on her face. "I had the pox," she told him.

"What an imagination this child has." Mr. Manetti chuckled. "And I thought you boys were supposed to be camping out."

"We were, Dad, but the ground is pretty hard," Tony told him.

"And it's getting cold outside," Matt said.

"And we got hungry," Hooter added, through a mouthful of guacamole and hot fudge sauce.

"You guys need to toughen up," Tony's father said, shaking his head. "What would you do if you were out in the wild and had to sleep on the ground?"

"Somehow I think we'd manage okay, Mr. Manetti," Matt told him.

"Yeah, Dad, we're tougher than you think." Tony grinned.

"So what are we looking up on the computer?" his father asked, leaning over to look at the screen. "Hmmm. 'Dorchester 1776,'" he read aloud. "That sounds interesting. Revolutionary War?"

The boys nodded. "It's for homework, Dad," Tony told him.

His father smiled. "Well, I'm glad to see you guys are doing your homework on a Friday night, rather than getting into trouble."

"Who, us get into trouble?" Tony said with an innocent look.

"Funny, but I don't ever remember reading about any battles in Dorchester," his father said, looking back at the computer screen. "Do any of you know what happened there?"

All four boys started talking at once.

"Hold on, hold on." Mr. Manetti laughed. "One at a time. You guys really seem to know your history."

The kitchen phone rang and Lily picked it up.

"Oh, hello, Mrs. Melrose," she said into the phone. "Yes, you can speak to Hooter. He's right here." She handed Hooter the phone.

"Hi, Mom! It's so good to hear your voice!" Hooter grinned. "Yes, I'm fine — I just miss you. . . . *Who* saw me running without my sneakers?" His smile faded as he looked down at his bare feet.

"Uh — well, no, actually I don't have them with me. I know where they are, though. It's kind of a long story. . . ."

Then Hooter held the phone at arm's length, and everyone could hear Mrs. Melrose shouting. "BRIAN MELROSE, I SWEAR THIS IS THE LAST TIME YOU ARE EVER GOING TO LOSE A PAIR OF . . ."

Matt and the others pressed their hands over their mouths to keep from laughing out loud.

"There's no place like . . ." Lily and Emma whispered together.

"Home," the others finished. "There's no place like *home*!"

Notes from the Author

THE LOYALISTS

In our story, Lily, Emma, and Katie were befriended and cared for by a Loyalist family living in Boston.

Although the Hewsons are fictional characters, they are based on some very real people of the time.

At the beginning of the American Revolution, there were 2.5 million people living in the colonies. More than five hundred thousand people (or over twenty percent of the American population) were driven from their homes during the war that gave birth to the United States. Although many of these people were born and raised in America, they were loyal to the King of England and were called Tories or Loyalists. While some of them fled to England, most escaped to Canada, where they became Nova Scotians, or Canadians. Many thousands of modern Canadians can trace their family trees back to the Loyalists of colonial America.

If you travel through eastern Canada today, into cities such as Halifax, Guysborough, Shelburne, and Manchester, you will see statues and plaques commemorating the Americans who resettled there. Shunned and ousted from their own country, these loyal supporters of the British Crown went on to face the hardships of creating new lives in a new land.

People from many different parts of colonial society pledged their allegiance to the King. Here are some examples.

Jon Joy was a Boston carpenter who led a crew of New England artisans, recruiting military carpenters for the King's forces in 1759.

Dr. John Jefferies became a physician to the British troops and treated many wounded after Bunker Hill.

Abraham Savage was a Boston tax collector turned supply officer to the King's men in the early part of the war.

Bartholomew Stavers was a postman from New Hampshire. In the summer of 1774 he was dragged out of his house and beaten for his outspoken loyalty to the Crown. His house was broken into and all of his furniture smashed. Bartholomew Stavers narrowly escaped death in his flight from the "rebel ruffians." He never returned to America.

Ben Franklin's own son, William, was a steadfast Loyalist during the Revolution. The close relationship William had with his father was broken over their disagreement about the colonies' right to freedom. William, who served from 1772 to 1776 as the last royal governor of New Jersey, was so loyal to King George that he is believed to have spied on Ben, feeding important information to the British authorities. William Franklin was arrested in 1776 and was held as a prisoner of war for two years before finally fleeing to the British-occupied city of New York and then on to England. He never returned to America.

Many Loyalists fled from one city to another in the colonies before they made the final break out of the country. Throughout the war, Loyalists poured into the British-occupied cities of Boston, Philadelphia, and New York, seeking the Crown's protection. The journey of these refugees was often long and hard and filled with uncertainty.

COLONIAL SPIES

In our story, Matt played a key role in Thomas Jamison's efforts to transfer information from the British lines in Boston to General Washington. Although Thomas and his ring of spies are fictional characters, they are based on a number of very real colonial spy rings.

Many individuals worked undercover throughout the Revolutionary War. These spies carried messages in hollowed-out buttons, shoe heels, quill pens, and even in bullets. It was a dangerous job for spies on both sides. Anyone caught spying by the English or Americans was hanged — sometimes without a trial.

One of the most famous spies to be caught carrying information for General Washington was a young rebel officer by the name of Nathan Hale. He was only twenty years old when he was caught and hanged in New York in 1776. His famous last words were, "I only regret that I have but one life to lose for my country."

General Washington's spies in Boston fed him information that led to the fortifications at Dorchester and the eventual retreat of British troops from the city.

Another successful spy ring was called the Clark Ring after its founder, Major John Clark. The Clark Ring, based in Philadelphia, fed General Washington critical battle plans during his stay at Valley Forge.

Another colonial spy ring, the Culper Ring, operated out of New York. This spy ring provided General Washington with valuable information that helped him win the war.

Women also played a role in American spying during the Revolution. Anna Strong and her clothesline were instrumental in the Culper Ring's success. By hanging a black petticoat on her line, Anna was able to signal to other members of the ring that an important message had arrived. She also worked out a code using handkerchiefs she hung to signal the times and places.

A young teenage girl by the name of Deborah Champion rode more than seventy-five miles in Connecticut to deliver secret messages to General Washington, who was waiting outside of Boston.

A New Jersey–born woman, Patience Wright, lived in England during the war. She was famous for the heads she sculpted out of wax and putty. It is believed that Patience Wright was also an active spy, concealing secret messages in her sculptures, which she shipped to key Patriots back in the colonies.

Waterproof ink was invented during the Revolutionary War. It lasted for months and proved quite handy in the harsh weather and rough terrain of the battlefields. Invisible inks invented in ancient times were also used. Messages written in these "disappearing stains" were hidden in everyday pamphlets, letters, or almanacs.

Both the Americans and the British used ciphers, or secret codes, to disguise important information crisscrossing enemy lines. Sometimes these codes used the rearrangement of letters, while other times they used numbers. Major Benjamin Tallmadge invented a secret code by using the numbers 1 through 763. For instance, the number 38 meant to attack, 192 stood for "fort," and 711 identified General Washington.

BOSTON IN 1776

In 1776, the city of Boston was in the grips of British occupation. The port was heavily monitored by English warships, and land access to the city was blocked. There were guards everywhere. These restrictions caused great hardship to the people of Boston. Fresh meat, milk, and other foodstuffs became scarce. There was little firewood for heat, and even hay for horses was hard to find. Smallpox had broken out. Many Patriots had left the city, while Loyalists from all over New England had poured in. Those Patriots still living in Boston were anxiously waiting for General Washington and his troops to come to their rescue.

LEECHES

Luckily for Katie, her brush with the bloodsucking leeches was narrowly avoided. But in colonial medicine the cure was often more frightening than the disease.

In 1776, the colonies had about 3,500 doctors, but of these only 400 had university degrees. Most physicians of the time learned their trade by working as apprentices. Little was known about germs and keeping wounds clean. Many soldiers died from minor wounds that became infected through dirt and bandages that were reused.

If you were unlucky enough to get shot by a musket ball, the procedure to remove it went something like this. An incision would be made with a sharp knife at the ball's entry. A special pair of tongs was then used to grip the ball and pull it out. The wound was wrapped in oil-soaked flannel, and this was topped by a dressing of milk and bread. Chances of infection were great. If the bullet didn't kill you, the infection that spread after it might.

Most colonial doctors believed in bleeding their patients in order to rid the body of bad humors. In addition to leeches, blood-sucking worms were also used to draw out blood.

A doctor of the time wrote about his work in these words:

> *When patients come to I*
> *I physics, bleeds,*
> *And sweats 'em.*
> *Then if they choose to die*
> *What's that to I — I lets 'em.*

One of the most deadly diseases in colonial America was smallpox. In 1777, George Washington ordered every soldier in his army to get immunized against the disease. There were no shots in those days. Instead, the doctors picked off the crust that had formed on the blisters of an infected patient. The doctor would then make a small cut in a healthy soldier's left shoulder and work the dried scab into the skin. The soldier was given a laxative, and this was followed by a bloodletting. The exhausted soldier was then made to rest in a special tent for a few days. It sounds awful, but it worked. Outbreaks in the army became few and far between.

George Washington himself suffered from poor health through most of his life. It is believed that he may have had tuberculosis, as well as having to suffer colds; ear, nose, and throat disorders; chronic coughs and shortness of breath; stomach and liver troubles; and carbuncles. He also had such terrible teeth that he had to endure many years of wearing a painful set of false teeth.

THE BATTLE OF DORCHESTER

There was a series of hills overlooking Boston harbor. It was here that Matt and his friends in the story went with the Patriots.

In real life, it was here that General Washington engaged in a maneuver that would outfox the British and ultimately set Boston free. By early March 1776, Washington's army had moved sixty tons of cannons and other weapons down from Ticonderoga to Cambridge. On March 4, General Washington ordered 2,000 of his troops up to the Dorchester Heights. They made their move under cover of night, with hay strewn on the paths up to the hills to muffle the sounds of their movements. All through the night, the rebels worked at building earthworks to overlook the city and harbor. They used trees, hay, mud, and rock-filled barrels to create an impressive line of defense that literally was built in a night. By four a.m. they had constructed fortifications that would amaze their enemy. General Howe was said to have exclaimed, "My God, these fellows have done more work in one night than I could make my army do in three months!"

After two hours of cannon fire by the British with no success against the fortifications, General Howe finally decided to retreat.

On March 17, 1776, 120 British ships, with more than 11,000 people aboard, sailed out of Boston's harbor. The siege of Boston was finally over. Of those fleeing Washington and his army, 9,906 were British troops, 667 were women, and 553 were children.

The departure of General Howe and his troops from Boston saw an end to any major military activities in the New England colonies for the remainder of the war.

Glossary

BAYONET: a pointed blade made to fit at the end of a musket or rifle

BOSTON COMMON: a large area of open shared land within the city limits of Boston

BREECHES: trousers that reach to the knee or just below it

CHAMBER POT: a pot or bowl used at night as a toilet that is kept under a bed

COBBLESTONES: stones used to make roads when cemented together

CURRENCY: money in current use

FLOGGING: a severe beating with a rod or whip

GOB: slang for "mouth"

GOUT: a painful inflammation usually of the big toe; believed to be caused by eating rich food

GUINEA: an English gold coin equal to 21 shillings; last minted in 1813

HARPSICHORD: a stringed musical instrument resembling a piano with two keyboards whose strings are plucked by either quills or points of leather

HIGHBORN: of noble birth; born into royalty

HUZZAH: a cheer or shout used to express joy or victory

LAD: a boy or man (affectionately)

LOBSTERBACK: colonial slang for British soldiers wearing red uniforms

LOYALIST: an American colonist who remained loyal to King George during the Revolutionary War; also known as a "Tory"

MUSKET: rifles used by American and British soldiers during the American Revolution

PATRIOT: an American colonist who fought against the King to form a new democratic country called the United States of America

PROVIDENCE: divine power that guides human destiny

REBEL: an American colonist who revolted against British rule

ROUND: a musical canon where one song is sung continually, but different singers begin at different times

SHILLING: a British coin worth 12 pence used prior to 1971

SHIN PLASTER: bandage
STOCKS: a wooden frame with neck, wrist, and ankle clamps used for public punishment

TORY: an American colonist who favored the English Crown during the American Revolution; also known as a "Loyalist"

Bibliography

Aron, Paul. *We Hold These Truths*. Lanham, VA: Rowman & Littlefield, 2008.

Bayne-Powell, Rosamond. *Housekeeping in the Eighteenth Century*. London: John Murray, 1956.

Bissell, Richard. *New Light on 1776*. Boston: Little, Brown, 1975.

Brands, H. W. *The First American*. New York: Anchor Books, 2000.

Brooks, Victor. *The Boston Campaign*. Conshohocken, PA: Combined Publishing, 1999.

Earle, Alice Morse. *Home Life in Colonial Days*. New York: Grosset & Dunlap, 1898.

Fraser, J. Walter. *Patriots, Pistols and Petticoats*. Charleston, SC: Charleston County Bicentennial Committee, 1993.

Isaacson, Walter. *Benjamin Franklin*. New York: Simon & Schuster, 2003.

Meltzer, Milton, ed. *The American Revolutionaries*. New York: Harper Trophy, 1987.

Moore, Christopher. *The Loyalists*. Toronto: Macmillan, 1984.

Pearson, Michael. *Those Damned Rebels*. New York: Putnam, 1972.

Raphael, Ray. *A People's History of the American Revolution*. New York: The New Press, 2001.

Rose, Alexander. *Washington's Spies*. New York: Random House, 2006.

Wilbur, C. Keith. *Revolutionary Medicine, 1700–1800*. Guilford, CT: Globe Pequot Press, 1980.

Wister, Sally. *Sally Wister's Journal*. Bedford, MA: Applewood Books, 1994 (1902).

GEORGE WASHINGTON'S SPY

Teaching Guide Available Online

www.scholastic.com/discussionguides